PARIS RED

ALSO BY MAUREEN GIBBON

Thief

Magdalena

Swimming Sweet Arrow

PARIS RED

a novel

MAUREEN GIBBON

W. W. NORTON & COMPANY

New York • London

Copyright © 2015 by Maureen Gibbon

All rights reserved
Printed in the United States of America
First Edition

For information about permission to reproduce selections from this book,
write to Permissions, W. W. Norton & Company, Inc.,
500 Fifth Avenue, New York, NY 10110

For information about special discounts for bulk purchases,
please contact W. W. Norton Special Sales at
specialsales@wwnorton.com or 800-233-4830

Manufacturing by Courier Westford
Book design by Ellen Cipriano
Production manager: Louise Parasmo

Library of Congress Cataloging-in-Publication Data

Gibbon, Maureen.
Paris red : a novel / Maureen Gibbon.—First edition.
pages cm
ISBN 978-0-393-24446-5 (hardcover)
1. Meurent, Victorine—Fiction. 2. Manet, Edouard, 1832–1883—Fiction.
3. Painters—France—Paris—Fiction. 4. Artists' models—Fiction. 5. Paris
(France)—History—1848–1870—Fiction. I. Title.
PS3557.I139167P37 2015
813'.54—dc23
2014034455

W. W. Norton & Company, Inc.
500 Fifth Avenue, New York, N.Y. 10110
www.wwnorton.com

W. W. Norton & Company Ltd.
Castle House, 75/76 Wells Street, London W1T 3QT

1 2 3 4 5 6 7 8 9 0

To be accurate is not to be right.

~SHIRLEY HAZZARD

That day I am seventeen and I am wearing the boots of a whore.

I wear the green boots of a whore and I stand with Denise outside a shopwindow. Behind the glass, scissors hang from hooks. Large shears on top, then a row of smaller scissors, then tin snips, pruning shears, pocketknives and switchblades. A few round silver plates and bowls mix in to break up all the sharpness. The man who owns the coutellerie told us he was from the Aveyron. The capital of knives, he says.

I stand in my bottle green boots and I am drawing a cat asleep on a shelf in the store window, just behind the *R* and the *E* of *Repassage Tous les Jours*. It is some cat, I think, to sleep so calmly among all the blades. The owner says he does not care that we stand there, drawing. We make people pause or stop by the store, which is fine by him.

So it is a white cat, the same white as the color of the letters on the shopwindow—except how do you draw white with a pencil? I consider that, guessing at how to draw the cat and what is around the cat, but it is not as if I know anything. Denise, either. But we draw anyway. It makes us unusual. Two girls with tablets and pencils. But Denise with her faraway eyes and me in the green boots of a whore, what we mainly draw is attention. I tell people that when they ask, and they laugh. But it is true. What I do not say is that drawing helps me see things, that it is a record of the day. Yet it is true, too.

So we stand outside the coutellerie and I am in my boots that are the color of grass, and I am trying to get the cat right as it goes on sleeping behind the *R* and the *E*, but my mind is elsewhere. I am looking at the cat and the scissors but in my mind I am thinking about my soldier, the one I stood kissing in the street the night before. The base of my tongue is still a little sore, that little ridge underneath, and I cannot help but run the tip of my tongue over the sore spot. It is peaceful to be standing next to Denise, absorbed in the cat but with my mind elsewhere, remembering the kiss. The soldier held me, and he leaned back against the stone of the building as we kissed. Even though the soldier was my cushion, I could feel the stone through his chest and his thighs. As if it were a wall in our own private room. I do not know how long we stood there. Long enough for the night to chill. But I was not cold and neither was he. At first his mouth tasted like him, at first he had a taste—smoke and alcohol and the taste of his mouth. But then his taste became my taste, and I could not tell us apart in the kiss.

"Look," Denise says. "It's going to stretch."

The cat opens its eyes a little and extends all four legs, pushing back against something invisible. Then it relaxes again. The only thing that changes is that the cat tilts its head to the side and shows the underside of its chin and throat.

"Now I have to change what I drew," Denise says.

So I look at my own pad, at the rounded shape I drew, and that is when I feel him. Not my soldier—a stranger.

He is standing somewhere behind me, off to the side. I feel him before I see him, and then I see him out of the corner of my eye. And I wonder how long he stood there, watching as I drew and daydreamed. Any other day I would have felt him as soon as he approached, would have felt him at my back and over my shoulder. But today I was thinking about my soldier and the way his thighs were like a cushion, and I did not feel the stranger approach. Was not aware of anything except my own sore tongue.

Behind my shoulder, in the vestibule of my eye—that is where I feel the stranger. He observes Denise and me the way we observe the cat.

But I am seventeen, in leaf green boots, and I know he will come over to us. And I know that when he comes over he will find a way to ask something. Anything.

And that is what he does. He moves out of the vestibule of my eye and he comes to stand beside us. He picks me to talk to, my shoulder to look over.

I know he has no interest in my pad or the shopwindow or the glob of a cat. I know it is just a way to stand close and begin talking. And I know that when he says *Pardon* and *May I*, that it is just a way to go on talking. But it is part of the reason Denise and I draw things: to be noticed, to be talked to. Because at the same time I know there is nothing at all special about me, I am seventeen and also know I am different from everyone else.

When he asks for the notebook, I give it to him. And when he asks for my pencil, I give him that, too.

"I'm no artist," he tells me when he takes my pencil.

I think about charming him. I think about telling him I have been drawing all my life. I think about saying how, when I was little, I used to beg pieces of charcoal from the coal man so I could draw on the pavement. But I do not say that. I do not say anything. Maybe because my tongue is sore and I am still thinking of my soldier. Or maybe because I know I do not have to say anything, and he will go on standing there. So I am silent and I watch him the way he watched me when he first came up and I didn't know he was there, when he was just a shadow in the corner of my eye.

He looks at the shopwindow and then looks down at my pad. In a moment he adds in shadows behind the cat. Which I would have done. But then he does something I would have not thought to do no matter how long I stood looking at the cat asleep on the shelf. After looking back at the store window, he adds a cross-hatched mark above the cat, up in the right corner.

It is a surprise, that mark. As soon as he makes it I cannot stop looking at it, and yet he did it without hesitation. Without thinking.

If I look at the crosshatched place one way, it looks like a smudge on the paper, but if I look at it another way, I see it makes the paper a window. The drawing now looks exactly like what it is supposed to be: a picture of a cat behind a glass window. Except that it is all on paper, and paper should not be able to look like glass.

"That did it," Denise says. "Now it looks real. Don't you think?"

She is right—without the crosshatched mark there is no window, and without the window, the picture makes no sense. And now I wish the cat was better. It looks all wrong, as if a child drew it. But I nod and say, "Ça marche."

Denise keeps turning her head to look at him, and by the way she holds her chin close to her shoulder I can tell she likes him. Likes the look of him. He is slender and has longish hair brushed back on the sides. He is older than we are but he stands with his shoulders back, the way a young man stands. I cannot tell exactly what his face looks like, not with the mustache and beard, but there is something raw about his eyes. They do not match the rest of his face, and he cannot hide them the way he hides his mouth, just as he cannot hide what he is doing, which is taking the time to stand talking to us. Girls in the street.

"How did you know to put it there?"

"What?"

"That shadow," I say, because I cannot stop looking at that spot, or how it has made the cat look flat, like an outline.

"It's just a reflection. That reflection," he says. He looks at the shopwindow and then looks back across the street to the pale building making the reflection.

As soon as he says it, I know that is the word I should have used—the mark is not a shadow at all. And I see what he means about the building across the way. But the shine of the building across the way is white, and the mark he made is gray, and it does not make sense to me. It does not make sense how a black pencil mark could show a white reflection. But it does. And then it comes to me: however white the reflection is, it is not as white as the paper. Nothing can be as white as the paper.

"The paper is the glass," I say.

I know he does not understand what I mean. The paper does not matter to him and the reflection does not matter to him—it was all just a way to take something from my hand, to go on talking to Denise and me. But he nods anyway, and that is when I know he is kind. At first I thought he was older but I see now he is not so old—it is just the beard and mustache, and the way his hair is carved away above his temples. His eyes are young and the skin around his eyes is young. I already know Denise likes him, so I decide to like him, too. That is how we pick him.

Or he picks us. I do not know. It does not matter.

I am still thinking of my soldier and the hard way he held me against him, but I choose this one, too. Because I am wearing the bottle green boots of a whore, because I am seventeen and I can choose who I like.

There on the street beside the shining knives, we all pick each other.

'm from Gennevilliers," he tells us at the small café down from the coutellerie.

He ordered for us, baba au rhum, and when the plates arrive, I glance at Denise. We both would have rather eaten a meal instead of dessert, but he invited us and is paying so there is no way to ask for it. Still, it is better than nothing, and when Denise will not catch my eye, I look away and begin eating.

"I've never been anywhere but here," Denise says.

"You could go to Gennevilliers. If you wanted. It isn't far."

"What do you do in Gennevilliers?"

"I'm a tax collector," he tells her, then gestures to our plates. "It's not enough, is it?"

At first I think he read my mind about the dessert, but just as quickly I realize it is not that at all, he is just watching us wolf down our food. So I make myself put my fork down as if I am getting full.

"It's delicious," Denise says.

I do not want to seem piggish, so I say, "I like it, too."

He smiles and looks away, into the smoke of his cigarette, to the other tables. And I wonder what we must look like to him. Both of us shiny-faced, in bad clothes, the ones we have worn for weeks, washing the armpits out in a basin in our room. But we are allowed to look like this—we are young. It is the only thing that matters. It is why he has brought us to a café, it is why he is sitting with us. It does not matter if our faces are oily or our dresses are thin. What matters is us, Denise with her dark hair and faraway eyes, and me with my red hair and bottle green boots. The other day, after my soldier and his friend bought us a drink, the friend kept pointing at us with his knuckle. *Rousse et brune,* he said. *Denise et Louise.*

You're mixing them up, my soldier said. *The brunette is Denise. Louise is the redhead.* But instead of pointing with a knuckle, he lifted his chin, first to Denise and then to me.

"Do you want coffee?" Eugène asks us now when he sees the waiter coming our way. Eugène—that is his name, or what he tells us is his name.

I do not even have to look at Denise. If he is going to spend any more money on us, we want some say in it. When we first sat down, we did not know which one of us he liked. I kept thinking it was me, but then he would turn his attention to Denise. And in a little while, I understand.

He likes both of us. The two of us, red and brown.

"I don't think so," I say. "I'd rather go for a walk."

A walk is free. No one is beholden to anyone for it, and at any point it can be broken off. If something does not please you, you use a corner and make excuses, which is easier to do if you are moving. Or you keep going, talking and dawdling. I walked with my soldier until I liked him well enough to kiss.

"That suits me," he says. He stubs out his cigarette and stands. Leaves some coins on the table.

Outside, he offers us each an arm. As we start to walk, Denise keeps the conversation going. I have words in my mouth, but they never seem right, and by the time I work out what to say, the conversation has moved on and I cannot say the thing I planned. So it is easier to be silent. To let myself go quiet and wait. I am just beginning to understand there is a power in being like that, in keeping things to myself. Yet without Denise it would be awkward. Without her I would have to talk.

"If he thinks life is so tragic, then he should kill himself," he tells Denise. "You know, kill yourself and stop pulling the rest of us down. Don't you think?"

They are talking about a play, I know that much, but when he turns to me for my answer, I just say, "No one needs any more sadness. It's better to laugh."

He looks at me as I say the words. I let him—I don't care if he knows I have not been listening. It does not matter to him. I see that. I have been holding his arm, walking beside him. Those things matter.

"I don't know," Denise says then. "Tragedy has a place."

"To hell with tragedy," he tells her. "Life is tragic enough."

The words that come out of his mouth—I know they are real and that he means them. But to me they are only sounds in the air. The only real thing is how his arm feels against my side. First there is the smooth cloth of his coat, but underneath I can feel muscle and even bone. He is slender but his arm is hard the way mine is not, the way a woman's cannot be. When we pass by people on the street, he draws Denise and me close to his sides, and that is how I begin to get a sense of him, of what it feels like to be close to him.

"///," he says then.

Denise laughs and looks at me. I missed whatever he said. Whatever it was that made her laugh like that.

"I'm sorry," I tell him. "What did you say?"

"You'll have to ask your friend."

"Nise, what did he say?"

"Oh. It's better coming from him, I think."

When I look at him this time, he is not smiling but his eyes are kind, and I know whatever he said was teasing—I know that. It is part of the game. He looks at me and then looks straight ahead again.

"I just said a little thing," he tells me then. "I just said I have one talkative wife and one silent wife."

When I hear his words, I know something happens in my face. I do not know what it is—I can only feel it inside. I know he is teasing but it still shocks me.

We go on walking then, but it is just a short way to La Maube, and when we get to the bottom of our street, Nise says, "This is us."

I do not know why she said anything—we could have gone on walking. But he lets go our arms. Any closeness I felt as he held my arm against his side is gone. I feel the loss in my hand and arm and along my side.

"Have dinner with me tomorrow," he says. But when Nise says *yes, we would like that*, he makes a point of looking at me.

"What about you?" he says.

"Yes, I would like to."

He kisses each of us then—a brush and a peck on the cheek—and tells us where to meet him.

That is how we leave him, in the doorway of the building on the corner of Maître-Albert, where the window says, *Enseignes Médailles Décorations Spécialité*. A stranger, except we do know his name.

All the way to our building I feel the loss of his arm and side along my arm and side. I feel it just as much as I can still feel my soldier's kiss. My body feels it.

"He's harmless," *Denise says when* we are back in our room, when we are getting ready for bed. She is already lying down but I am still standing, washing my face with a wet cloth.

"I don't know," I say. "What does he want?"

"What do you think? He called us his wives. He wants to sleep with us."

When I do not answer, Nise says, "What? You don't think so?"

"I don't know. He's not in a rush about it."

"He's bored. He has time on his hands."

"Maybe," I say.

"I liked him. I thought he was handsome."

"So see," I say. "Maybe he's not so harmless."

"We don't even have to go if we don't want to," she tells me then. "I just meant he doesn't have to be anything to us."

I want to say, *No one has to be anything to anyone, that's the problem.* But I do not. And when I go on not saying anything, I hear Nise move on the bed.

"So you don't want to go?" she asks.

"What, and miss dinner?"

She snorts then, the way I mean her to do, and I crawl into bed, too.

But there is something that keeps turning itself over and over inside me. I keep thinking about the way he looked at me before he said, *I have one talkative wife and one silent wife.* It bothered me when he said it, and it still bothers me. I thought I understood why, but now I do not.

I go on thinking in the dark, waiting to hear or feel Nise move, listening for her breath to change when she falls asleep, but it sounds like she is still awake. Maybe she is thinking about him, too. Maybe both of us are thinking of him and pretending to sleep.

So I try to think about my soldier. I do not remember things the right way, though, and when I climb inside the thoughts to make myself feel the kiss again, it seems faint, and I can hardly feel it. And when I do fall asleep I am not thinking about my soldier but of him. Of him and Nise and me.

W*e live at 17 Rue* Maître-Albert, just at the elbow in the street. The room is furnished with one bed, a deal table, a spidery chair, and a washbasin on an old dresser. We use my trunk as a nightstand, and the first thing I see when I wake up is the blue box of La Favorite candles we keep there. *Exiger le nom,* the box says. *Brûlant sans huile, 8 Heures, Lacorre Frères, Paris.* Except the box doesn't look blue, it looks gray. In the early morning light, things still have not regained their color: not the box of candles, not the dark maroon paint someone used on one wall, not the dirty white of the other walls, not my blue dress or Nise's brown one—not even my green boots. Everything is gray or black, or a shade of gray or black.

So the room is shit. But at least it has a window. High up—I have to stand on my toes to see out—but it is a window. And if I get up on one of the beat-up chairs and stick my head out, to the right I see Maison Perrier, the Quai de la Tournelle, and the river itself. Directly across the street is the shop that hangs out brushes and brooms and baskets, and if I could somehow see around the corner, around the dogleg the street makes and down to Place Maubert, I would see my favorite shop. *Bois et Charbon*, the sign for the shop says, but it is the little painted plaques they have all over the front of the building that I like so much. The plaques show cut logs, all sorts of trees, and leaves in every shade of green. The owner stands outside sometimes in his vest and apron, and I do not know which is blacker, his pelt of a beard or his eyes.

That shop is like a forest in the city.

But I do not go to the window just yet. I lie in bed and look at the colors that are not colors and the box of candles. *Combustion parfaite.* I want to touch the sore place at the base of my tongue so I can remember the soldier's kiss, but I think of what happened the night before so I do not. I do not want to lose the feeling of the kiss altogether. Or maybe it is already lost and I do not want to know. Instead I remember the way I kept my hand up by the soldier's mouth when we kissed. I felt the way he hungrily bit me. I felt it with my mouth but also with my fingertips.

Last night's kiss was nothing. A soft moment when lips pressed against my cheek. Men's mustaches and beards usually smell of smoke and their dinners, but the kiss he gave on the street was so swift I only felt the brush, and there was no smell at all. But I remember the way his eyes looked as he came in close to me. That is the thing that keeps going through my mind.

Nise turns then in the bed, pulls her pillow close with her hand. I see that out of the side of my vision just before I close my eyes. I do not want her to know I have been up, thinking—it is my bit of privacy. I used to have to block her out entirely to sleep because I did not like the feeling of sharing such a small space with anyone, not even someone I knew well, but it is not that way anymore. I can be private in my mind and be right next to her. And I know her better. I thought I knew her before but I did not. Now she is like a sister to me. She has:

A faint brown birthmark on her back that looks like a small island.

A tiny triangle of space between her thighs when her legs are closed, just below her sex.

An eye that looks off to one side just the slightest bit.

When she looks straight at me, it seems as though she is looking at me and seeing me but also seeing something just over my shoulder. As if there were a little bit of space around me that only she can perceive. I have watched people study her and try to understand what is wrong with her eye, but then they stop. They accept her gaze as part of the prettiness of her face, and in a little while they begin to feel that bit of space around them, too. They grow calm and kind. If her eye turned inward it would be a flaw, but as it is, it makes her face unique.

It is always the flaw that interests me.

And she could tell you intimate things about me, too. Like how I sometimes sleep with one hand between my legs to keep my fingers warm, or how I have a single, fine reddish-blonde hair that grows beside my right nipple. I pluck it out as soon as I can pinch it between my fingers. I used to try to hide that from Nise, and do it when she wasn't looking, but then I thought, why bother?

You get to know someone pretty well when you share a bed and a slop bucket.

When I open my eyes this time and look at the box of candles, I can see the blue is just starting to come back to it. I try to watch the color come back degree by degree, but it makes my eyes hurt to study it that way. It is easier to look away and then look back. By now I have watched the box so long it would not surprise me if it began to move, if it lifted off the trunk and into the air. And I think that is how the world should work. If you think about things hard enough, you should be able to will them to do what you want. And maybe things do work that way. Maybe I just have not learned to think hard enough.

Inside the trunk the box of candles is resting on, there is next to nothing. Two pillowcases my mother made me embroider when I was a girl, and a coppery scarf with most of its fringe missing. Also a gift from the whore. She gave the scarf to me the same day she gave me the green boots. She found out I had been sick when she came by to pick up the sewing she hired my mother to do, and she asked my mother if she would be offended by a few hand-me-downs. My mother said no, that she would be glad for anything to distract me.

"The boots are too loud," she told my mother and me the day she brought the things she wanted to give me. "They don't go with anything. And the scarf is sad."

Her whore name was La Belle Normande, but I knew her real name. Julie. Whenever I saw her on the street, I admired her clothing—a blue dress and a gold one, a garnet coat. I was ten and could not understand why she would not want the green boots.

"They're too gaudy," she said. "Même pour moi."

"I like them," I told her after I put them on and buttoned them up. But when I tried walking in them, my foot slid all the way forward, and the heel of my foot was nowhere near the heel of the shoe.

"Maybe you can play dress-up with them," Julie said. "Do you play dress-up?"

There were no extra clothes in the house, just my mother's things that she wore every day, and a black lace mantilla she sometimes wore for church. A couple of times when I was little I put it on over my hair. So I told Julie, "I used to play dress-up. Sometimes."

"Then the boots are yours. Along with the sad scarf."

Now the boots fit me. I think the color goes with everything, the way grass goes with sky and flowers and dirt. Even when the leather gets damp, the color does not change. It is still emerald. As if I would know what an emerald looks like, but in my mind I know the stone must look something like my boots. What I know for certain is I am always sure of myself when I wear the boots, the way I was sure of myself yesterday when I felt him standing just behind my shoulder, when I was sure he would come over to talk to us. Maybe that is the way to will things to happen: not to think hard about things to get them to happen but to be so sure of them that they do happen.

Or maybe what happened yesterday was just this: when one man likes you, others do, too. It is like a smell you carry on your skin, or a look that changes your face. Maybe I was standing differently on the street yesterday because of how long I stood kissing my soldier the night before. Maybe my daydreams of kissing my soldier changed the way my face looked as I stood outside the coutellerie and drew that lump of a cat.

I rub the tip of my tongue over the base again and now it does not ache at all. Already the soldier is fading. But I tell myself it does not matter because the next thing has begun to happen.

"Why are you up so early?" Denise asks then from the bed. She is waking up, stretching her legs, pushing out with the palms of her hands into the air. Stretching just the way the cat in the window did. "What's the story?"

She would listen if I told her—she always does. But she would also tease me for waking up early to daydream about my soldier or about the new one. She would say, *They're just men.*

So I shake my head. "No story," I tell her. "Just the day."

he next night he takes us for dinner to a place off one of the boulevards. Nicer than anything on La Maube, but what wouldn't be. The point is it is not La Maube, but it is still not so nice as to make a person feel odd.

"You don't live in Gennevilliers," Denise says after we sit down. "You know the streets too well. Is this your neighborhood?"

"I only said I was from Gennevilliers," he says.

"You're not a tax collector, either, are you?" she asks.

"Maybe I'm a glass blower from Venice. Does it matter so much?"

"Maybe it does," Denise says. "Do you want us to believe the things you tell us?"

"You should believe what you want. My brother-in-law is a tax collector. Is that enough?"

"Is what you told us even your real name? Eugène?"

"For now," he says. "It will do for now."

But he is not angry at her for asking, and when I see that, I understand something. He wants us to be his equals. We have to be his equals in some way or there is no point. He could buy a woman if he wanted that. It is something different he wants from us. With us.

Nise says, "Well, if you can lie, we can, too. It goes both ways."

"You're both what, eighteen? You don't have to lie."

"I'm nineteen," Nise tells him.

"Still."

"Everyone has to lie," I say. It is the first thing I have said after he kissed us each hello and brought us into the restaurant. I do not correct him to tell him I am seventeen, and I do not look away when he turns to me. I let him look at me.

"My silent wife," he says.

I tell myself the word sounds silly. I tell myself that it is all a game. That is what I see in his face. Nise and I are an amusement to him, a pastime. In his coat and tie, what else could we be? But if we are a game for him, it is also true that he would like us to play with him. Wants us to play with him. I see that in his eyes, in the plum shadows beneath his eyes. But I do not turn away, will not turn away, and in the end he is the one who looks down to his cigarettes.

"You can be Eugène," I tell him. "If we get to pick our names, too."

"What names do you want?" he asks.

"You have to let us think," Nise says. "No, I know. I'm Pâquerette."

"Pâquerette," he says, shaking his head. "Of course. It's ridiculous. What about you?"

"Victorine," I say.

"Victorine?"

"Not like that," I say. "Not fancy. Vic'trine. Maybe just Trine."

"Straightforward."

"That's right."

"Not sweet like Daisy."

"That's right."

"Now we're getting somewhere," he says, and picks up a menu. "Order what you want. No soupe aux choux tonight, or whatever you're used to down on La Maube."

He says it to tease us, but it is true enough. Except we live on less than cabbage soup sometimes, less than even what he imagines. There is no place to cook in our room, and even if there were, we would not. We eat fritters at lunch and whatever we can bring home to our room for dinner. We do not sit down in cafés, not even for thin soupe aux choux. We eat in our room or on the street.

"We don't go hungry," I say. "We've never gone hungry."

"I didn't think so."

What I meant is there is a difference between going hungry and wanting more. Between having something and having enough. But somehow everything at the table changes then, as if there is a wire connecting the three of us. Almost as if we are touching knees under the table. But we are not touching. It is just the three of us sitting, and everything alive in the space between us. Maybe just because I used the word *hungry*, which is another way of saying *want*.

But all he says is, "Order what you like." And nods at the menu.

We eye the list of truite à la Vénitienne, poulet à la Singarat, filet de boeuf Richelieu and something à la printanière. Then, we order not just enough, but enough to fill us.

So that is the first thing he gives us. Bellies tight and round as drums.

～

Sometime during the meal I take a long time to study him. I thought I knew what he looked like the day we met him, but I did not. He was not a person to me then, and I could only see what I thought he was. This is what he really looks like:

Nose crooked, the bridge going off to the left and the tip to the right. But it is a fine-tipped nose, with elegant nostrils, if you can say such a thing. Hazel irises that look pale because of his deep-set eyes. One vein that shows slightly under the skin of his forehead. Deep lines carved down to the corners of his mouth. There is something fine-grained about his face in spite of the riotous beard and mustache. He would look younger without them, but he wants to hide behind them.

He wears a black coat, pale clay-colored pants. At first I thought his vest was black, too, but it is not. It is dark purple, sister of black, the darkest shade there is, skin of blackberries. Why that and not plain black? How much money and how much trouble to buy a color instead of black? It must matter to him. But why?

His tie is dotted. Held with one pin whose head is a dull, red stone. A garnet? A ruby? To me it is the color of jam.

In all he could not be more different from my soldier, and just thinking that makes me remember the soldier's kiss and the salty way his skin tasted when I put my mouth on his collarbone.

But by then he has seen me looking, studying him.

"Do I pass?" he asks.

"You do all right," I say.

He watches me for a second—maybe he can see what I was thinking, maybe he knew I was thinking of what my soldier's skin tasted like. Yet if he could see what I was thinking about my soldier, then he must know what else passed through my mind: that I've held his arm in mine through the streets, that I already am beginning to imagine what it is like to be with him.

Neither of us moves—not him toward me or me toward him—and he turns back to Nise. He does not even go on looking at me. But that is when I feel the wire between the two of us get a little tighter.

Just a little tighter.

Somehow during dinner it comes out that we work not so far from there, on Rue Pastourelle.

"That's how we met," Nise tells him. "In the big Baudon workshop room."

"What's Baudon? What exactly do you do?"

"We're *brunisseuses*. Silver burnishers."

"You polish silver?"

"That's the last step," I say. "We're the step before. We ground the silver plate onto the metal."

"How much does that pay?"

I know he is just curious, but I do not feel like saying. When I look over at Nise, I know she feels the same.

"It pays better than some jobs," she says.

He nods and takes Nise's hand and runs his thumb over her fingertips, and then he takes my fingers with his other hand.

"You'll have to walk me by there after dinner," he says. "By Baudon."

"I don't think so," Nise tells him. "We see enough of the place during the week."

"There's nothing to see anyway," I say.

"How many girls in your workshop?"

"Twenty-four? Twenty-five? Some come and go."

"That would be something to see," he says. "Two dozen girls working."

"They aren't all girls. Some are women and some are old hags," Nise says. "I've been there since I was fifteen."

"I've been there a little more than a year," I tell him.

He does not say anything then, just keeps our fingers in his hands.

"What, did you think we just went around drawing, picking up men?" Nise asks. Teasing. She looks down at her plate when she says it, but then she raises her eyes to look at him, to see his reaction.

There are plenty of whores. Or what people call whores. A girl we know, Marie Mousseau, got picked up in bed with two firemen. Her landlord gave her up. But she was a cook. We saw her go to work, we saw her at work. If she was just a whore, why would she bother cooking and cleaning up in a shitty café on La Maube? So money changes hands because one person has more and one has less. Why call it anything?

"I knew you worked," he says then. "I didn't know at what. I just wondered how you got on."

"As an apprentice, you go three months without pay," I say. "Then you get a franc a day. Now we get ten francs a week."

Each of our dinners will cost 1.50 francs, the prix fixe, plus the wine. I start adding, then multiplying. I want to say, we do not make much, but it is enough to live on. I want to say we are with him because we choose to be, because he interests us. That if he had been someone else—crude or boorish, or if we did not like the smell of his hair or the way he wore his jacket—we would have never said yes. That one thing does not mean another.

He rubs his fingers over the pads on my palm, then over my fingers again.

"I can tell you both do the same job. You have calluses in the same places," he says, and gives us back our hands.

⚜

At the end of the meal, when he goes to pay the check, he pulls a handful of coins from his pocket, but that is not the thing I notice. What I notice is how, after he counts out the ones he wants, he lets them fall to the table. He does not lay out the coins, he does not present them. He opens his fingers and—how can I say it? Both drops and tosses them to the table. One small flip, hardly a motion at all, and the coins lay where they fall.

Then the money-holding hand brings everything that is left back to his pocket.

I have never had a coin that I did not finger carefully or part with reluctantly. Never dropped money or tossed it with a small flick of the fingers. Never brought a jingling handful of coins back to my pocket or a purse.

Of course he knows how to do all those things. He does not know he knows, but he does all the same.

fter dinner we go out walking on the boulevard. We walk three abreast again, Nise and me on either side of him.

"We're some kind of slow-moving animal," I say, swaying into him.

"One with three heads," Nise says, and I feel her sway into him.

He can feel her breast against one arm and mine against the other.

"We're our own kind of animal," he tells us.

Yet it is not awkward to walk that way. Sometimes people have to make room for us, but they do. It is not just the space we take up, I think, that makes people notice us—it is our slow pace. It gives them time to look and understand. To make up the story of the three of us as they pass us by.

Walking, I remember what his arm felt like from the last time, but he still is not familiar. He still feels like a stranger against my side. A stranger I can touch, who holds me close. It is that part I like best, being so close to someone and not knowing him, still coming to know him. But while we walk I keep feeling there is something familiar about him, something I recognize, and in a little while I realize what it is.

His scent.

Not just the cigarette smell or the smell of the cloth of his jacket, but something else I cannot yet name. And once I get that in my mind, it occupies me so much I cannot say anything at all, not even the occasional comments I try to make just to show I am listening, that I am not just a mute body, a breast pressed up against his arm. A silent wife. When he turns to me, I am sure that is what he will say.

"Don't go away from us," he says instead. Shakes my arm a little in his.

"I'm just thinking," I say.

"What of?"

"Of my mother."

"Like a baby," Nise says, and laughs a little.

He smiles but does not laugh. Holds my arm a little tighter to his side.

I do not say that it has just come to me that his smell makes me think of the clove-studded orange I helped my mother make one Christmas. When we first stuck the pointed ends of the cloves into the orange, the smell was so sharp it seemed to burn my nose, and the whole orange smelled raw. But over the days, that burning went away and the orange scent got fainter and the cloves got warmer, and soon all you could really smell was cloves.

He smells of smoke and cloves. But I do not say that, I only say, "It doesn't make any sense, I know."

We go on walking, past cafés that shed so much light into the street you can see everything as clearly as day, past a column with posters that advertise:

THE PETITE MARIÉE WITH JEAN RAISIN
AT THÉÂTRE DE CLUNY

CENDRILLON AT THE CIRQUE D'HIVER

BAL BULLIER.

A little further on, we pass a kiosk in the square that sells jumping ropes, hoops, puppets, tops, balls, tiny baskets—all manner of cheap toys. Closed now, but when I passed it the last time, it was run by a heavyset woman in a black bonnet trimmed with white lace. And I think the thing I always think when I pass by: did I ever have toys like that? Cheap things meant to last a short time, bought on impulse? If I did, I don't remember.

And there above the shuttered windows of the kiosk I see the sign. In white letters on black.

DEMANDEZ DU PLAISIR.

And I am thinking of those words and how we all want plea-sure, how we are born wanting something to hug and something to play with and something to finger and something to suck. How it is one thing when you're young and something different when you get older, but the wanting does not change. I am thinking of all of that, and maybe he and Nise are, too. Maybe they saw the sign and believe it was meant for them just the way I believe it was meant for me.

I am thinking all that when we come around the corner and see the girl standing outside the market. The place is closed for the day, but she is selling paper cones of cherries, the first of the season, to the couples and fancy people walking by. She has two cones left so he buys them, and Denise takes one cone and I take the other, and we find a place to sit.

We eat the sweet cherries, which are the same color, I think, as the stone in his tie pin. Denise offers her cone to him and then I do, and the three of us eat. We slip the pits into our fingers and then toss them onto the ground.

There is not that much fruit in the cones, and when I get to the last cherries, I take the stem of one with my first two fingers and my thumb. I hold the cherry by its stem so the fruit rests against the soft part of my thumb, and then I move my hand close to his mouth so he can eat it.

And he does. He leans forward a little and bites the cherry from its stem.

I feel the softness of his lips and mustache on my thumb, and then I feel him kiss around the fruit and through the fruit to my skin.

Nise watches at first. She could do it too if she wanted—he made it clear that he wants to treat us equally. But she does not offer him a cherry to eat from her hand. Instead she looks away and just goes on eating, finishing the fruit in her cone.

I have two cherries left, and I hold each one up for him. Each time he bites, he kisses. Makes my palm a mouth. That is all I can think of, there on the bench. I stop thinking about Nise being beside him. I do not think about anything except his mouth on my skin.

I could lean toward him, I could get him to kiss my mouth instead of my thumb—I know I could. But I do not let myself because of Nise. Whatever it is that has started includes her, and even though she is not feeding him, she is there. She is there beside him, too. So as much as I would like to kiss him, I do not. I let my hand be a mouth.

It seems as if he eats cherries from my hand for a long time.

When we stand up to walk again, I feel bound to him, and I also feel something taut in the skin of my wrist and hand. And even though I did not kiss him, I still feel a little guilty. Because I wanted to be there with him alone, because I wanted him for myself. To myself. And if we had gone on sitting there much longer I would have kissed him. I would have kissed him and would not have cared if Nise was beside us or not.

As we walk, I look at Nise to see if she knows how I feel. But I do not see any sign that she is upset or that she has hurt feelings. Maybe she is hiding it, but she talks to him as easily as before. Teasing and sweet. And then I understand I got it wrong.

She turned away from him and me to give us our privacy, the way she and I turn away from each other in our room. That is all.

So the three of us still walk arm in arm in arm, a three-headed, three-hearted animal, and when we get back to Maître-Albert, Nise is the one who says, "You can come home with us. You don't have to go all the way to Gennevilliers. Or wherever it is that you live."

He stops and looks at her.

"From what you tell me, there's hardly room for the two of you," he says. "Where would you put me?"

This time I am the one who speaks. "In our bed," I tell him.

Now I am the one he looks at, and I can see from his face that I have pleased him. Nise pleased him with her offer and I have pleased him with the quickness of my reply. I see the pleasure in his eyes as he steps close to me.

"Brava," he says.

It is not a real kiss he gives me then, but it is still slower than the brush the night before, and there is a little moisture on his lips. I feel his lips and the soft mustache I felt on my hand, but there is a pressure in the kiss as well, a kind of intent. An insistence.

When he pulls back from me, he turns to Denise. Because he needs to keep it fair, because we have all been walking arm in arm, because her breast has been mashed against his arm just as mine has. So he kisses her, too, and I watch. The brown wing of her hair and her closed eyes. The way the back of her jaw curves upward. The careful way he leans in.

And the thing I have been understanding about him all night becomes clear just then. He likes to be teased. He likes for us to play with him. It is part of what he wants from us.

We make plans to meet the day after tomorrow, and that is

how we leave him, that is how we part on the street. With the feeling of his mouth on both of our mouths.

Maybe that is why Nise and I do not talk for the last half a block, from the corner of La Maube to the elbow of Maître-Albert. We want to keep the feeling of his mouth on our mouths. There is nothing to say just then, anyway.

"*knew he wouldn't come*," *Nise* says as she scrubs her face back in our room. "That's why I could ask him."

"He liked that you asked."

"Did he?"

"You know he did," I say. "And I just followed up on your invitation."

I am tired but I am also wide awake. Aware. I feel something from Nise, but I cannot trace it, not just yet.

"It's awkward, isn't it," she says then.

"What is?"

"The three of us. Waiting like that to be kissed. I had to look away when he was kissing you."

I nod because I do understand. In the past when we met men, there was always one for her and one for me. Always. But in another way I do not know what she means at all because tonight he kissed me first. I did not have to wait. And when he kissed Nise, I watched. I made a point not to look away.

"Do you like him more than you thought you would?" she asks.

"I don't know," I say.

I do know, but it is too soon to talk about. And I think she must feel the same because she does not ask or say anything else about him. When she speaks again, it is about work the next day.

"When do we ever want to go?" I say.

When we get in bed, I listen for Nise breathing and keep trying to hear the change, the passing from wakeful lying there to sleep. It is the quietest change, but some nights I am still awake when it happens, and when I hear it, it soothes me. Tonight I want to lie in the darkness, being soothed by Nise's breathing, want to look at my green boots across the room, which now seem black, at the blue box of candles, which has now turned gray. *Exiger le nom. Éviter les contrefaçons. La Favorite.*

But I do not hear the change in her breathing tonight, at least not that I can tell, and when I fall asleep I am thinking of the way his mouth felt on the nest of veins in my wrist, and Nise is the one awake. Or so it seems to me.

orure Argenture Plaquage. That is what the sign for
Baudon says. We do not go in the front door under the sign,
though—we walk around to the side courtyard and go through a
blue door that slides open on a pulley and chain.

To burnish silver plate, you do not rub it with cloth—hard
needs hard. I use a thin steel tool, the tip a third the width of a
finger, to ground the silver, and then I use a tool with a wider tip
to blend out all the edges. The tools are called almost the same
thing as the workers: *brunissoirs.* I use shop tools for everything
but the last wide, feathering strokes—that is when I use my own
burnisher. The tip is bloodstone, not steel. The stone is as wide as
my thumb, set in a forked wooden handle, and held in place with a
steel band. Bloodstone is not red like its name but shiny gray, the
color of river water in sunlight. I can see myself in it, and it is the
mirror of the bloodstone that makes a mirror of the silver.

Whenever I am not using my burnisher, I keep it in its own leather pouch. If anything scratches the stone, that scratch will start to pull on the silver and ruin anything it touches. Baudon is a clean shop with good enough tools, but I know the feeling of my own burnisher and it knows me. I know the way the stone slips out over the grooved edges of grounded silver, I know the way I can steady the handle with my little finger, and I know the smooth feeling of the wooden end in the center of my palm. It is my tool and I know it better than I have ever known any man's cock—that is what I am saying.

I got the importance of tools from my father. He is an engraver, a ciseleur, with his own set of burins, and he told me you could not be anybody until you had your own tools, whatever your trade. When I was growing up, my mother screamed about whatever boy I was running around with, but my father worried about how I would make a living.

I guess they each worried in their own way, but I cannot help that it was my father's lessons about tools that I took to heart.

There is a beauty to the burnishers, each one with its own tip and own purpose. Sometimes I want one of the old-time dog's tooth burnishers. Some of the gold workers at Baudon use them, though most have switched to agate. But not all. Those dog's tooth burnishers are just what they are called—the curved eyetooth of a dog is set in the end of a wood handle. You do not use them on silver, only on gilt, but I would like one for myself all the same. A dog's tooth, a piece of bone set in wood.

As I said, Baudon's not bad. We even have work in August when everything shuts down. And the shop does not scrimp.

Silver plate can be as thin as a scraping of butter, but the thinner the deposit, the grainier the matte finish is and the harder you work. Not Baudon. They are not cheap.

Burnishing makes your hands ache but also the muscles in your back, too, right beneath the shoulder. That is where the strokes come from—it is not just your fingers doing the work, but your back, too. Sometimes it feels like someone is poking me with a hot needle or a knife. The spot that burns the worst is just below the shoulder blade on my right side, just to the right of my backbone. The spot where a wing would be if I were a bird. But I am not a bird, just a working girl, and sometimes that spot feels like fire.

⚓

At times during the day it seems like everyone in the shop is talking, and the place is loud with conversations and shouts across the tables. Other times, first thing in the morning or midafternoon, the place goes quiet and you hear the click-click-clicking of the burnishers going over the silver. Nise and I do not work at the same table—we see enough of each other is what we always tell people. So she gets the gossip from her end of the room and I get it from my end.

Those quiet spots in the days, or times when people are just talking quietly as they work, doing the same things over and over—they can almost put you to sleep. The murmuring sound of women talking and the steady sound of plates and bowls being rubbed by our tools—it lulls. Sometimes it seems the whole place is muffled, even though it is filled with metal, and that is when I can think best. When my hands are doing something but I cannot really make out what anyone is saying about what their husbands did, or who is pregnant or what happened the night before. That is when it seems like I am rubbing out the ridges of my own thoughts with my stone.

Today I think about how it probably only makes sense that each of my parents worried the way they did. They knew they could not control me. The first night I stayed out all night with a boy I was just fifteen. When I did come home, my father had already gone to work, but my mother was sitting there. When I walked in that morning, I said, "I'm back. I'm back now." But she would not answer. She would not talk or look at me. And when she finally did talk, she said, "If you come home pregnant, you won't be my daughter."

As if I would want a child. As if that were not something I wanted to avoid, too. She could have helped me with it, she could have helped me learn how not to, but she did not.

I got over the boy I stayed out all night with, and in the end I did not even care for him, but it was never the same between my mother and me. I never forgot her not speaking to me, or the way she would not even turn her head to look at me. She gave me the side of her face. That was all.

So I grew up. Even though I lived at home for another few months, that was the day I began to leave. And my father's way was better: he did not hold things against me, and he made sure I knew I needed my own tools. Though maybe by not helping me, by forcing me to find out things on my own, my mother did the same.

We wear big aprons over our dresses in the shop, and that is what Nise and I are rolling into bundles when we walk out into the street at the end of the day. We are hanging the aprons over our shoulders by their strings the way we always do when we see him.

Except I do not see him at all at first—Nise does. It is the change in how she walks that makes me look across and down the street.

He is leaning against the building on the corner of the street, smoking. When he sees us, he drops his cigarette and glances down to step on it once. Then he looks at us again. He does not walk toward us—he lets us take him in. Lets us decide how we want to proceed.

"Is that what you caught?" Adèle asks us.

She is a little older than we are, works at the table next to Nise, and she sees where we are looking and who we are looking at. I glance over at Adèle and see the expression on her face, but for once she does not say anything loud or rude. Does not even stop moving. She is going home to her husband and her baby, and she does not care who is waiting in the street to see us. She is someone to gossip with to make the day go quicker. A work friend.

When we get closer, I see he is dressed poorer than we have

seen him before: dark pants and some shapeless coat. But it does not matter. Even if he thinks he has disguised himself, there is no way he fits in here where people have worked all day among the metal and rags and sawdust and heat and dirt. I want to laugh at him but I do not, and in another second I am there in front of him and I do not want to laugh. I look at him full on, but Nise stands off to the side. He just goes on waiting, watching us, letting us be the ones to decide.

"What, have you come down in the world?" Nise asks him, turning to him for just a second. Acknowledging him.

"I was around," he says. "In the neighborhood."

She shakes her head, and rewraps her apron so it is like a muff in front of her. "In this neighborhood. On this street. After we told you where we worked," she says straight ahead, into the air, not turning toward him again.

She will not look at me, either, so I do not know exactly what she is feeling, but I know how I feel. Caught out somehow. We are in our work clothes with dirty hair, and there is something odd about all of it. I think about the way he threw the cigarette down as soon as he saw us, how he toed it out almost without looking away from us. And yet he stood there so we could have time to think. To decide.

It makes me wonder who is hungry, really.

I do not wrap my hands in my apron the way Nise does—my apron is still hanging in a bundle from my right shoulder. It dangles between me and him as the three of us set off down the street. He walks with his hands behind his back. And we go for a block like that. Not talking. But before too long I find myself drifting closer to him. Even though we are not touching, I feel connected to him.

"I missed my working girls," he says then. "With the calluses on their hands."

No one says anything then but I see Nise turn toward him once, and her face looks miserable. That is when I understand that she is embarrassed about our filthy hands and dirty dresses and the stink of our armpits and about being caught out like this. And I see something else in her face, too, and I think it is this: that whatever he is doing with us is more real now because he has come to our work, because he has come to us in the daylight. Because he stood in the street and watched for us. It is not just about him buying us a couple of dinners or teasing with made-up names and stories.

It is about us. Something specifically about us. And I think we should not be surprised. It is what we wanted. With our tablets and our scheming, all the trying not to be ordinary—didn't we want someone to notice us? To see we were different? Isn't that why I wear the green boots of a whore? Because I do not feel ordinary. Or because I feel ordinary and different at the same time.

That is when I decide I am not upset anymore about being caught off guard at Baudon, or even about his pretend shabbiness—as if you could put a life on with a coat. I bring myself back, I focus on the street and walking beside him. And in a little while I slip my hand in the crook of his arm. I do not walk as close to him as I have at night—there is the bundle of apron between us and the daytime. And that is the thing: it is not night-time, it is daylight and the front of my dress is still damp with the crocus martis and soap suds we use when we are burnishing, and I stink in the exact sharp way that comes from working in the heat of the shop. I am not wearing the green boots of a whore, I am not drawing in a notebook, I am not eating a fancy meal or listening to made-up names.

I am my daylight self.

Yet I am not just myself, either, because I became something different the day I met him. Just the way I became something different when I kissed my soldier, or when I stayed out all night with a boy against my mother's wishes. I keep changing. Keep wanting to change.

Girls with rough hands in dirty dresses—that is what he wants. Not the story we made up for ourselves in the restaurant, not anything pretend. That is what I understand on the street.

～✿～

When we sit in the café off the Boulevard du Temple, he seems different somehow.

I think at first maybe it is just the clothes changing how I see him, but in a little while I am sure it is more. He slides down in his chair, his words sound loose, and even the tone of his voice is altered. It is a little deeper somehow, and slower. I listen and watch for a while and then I think, he is like me, he alters for the occasion.

After we get our wine, we sit with the *Journal Pour Tous* that he brought, looking at the pictures. He lets us leaf through it for a while and then he shows us the drawing he said made him think of us. It is titled "Langage des Cheveux," and it shows the heads of four different women. There is no color in the newspaper, but the hair colors are shaded differently, and each of the women is labeled: blonde, noire, rousse, brune. Underneath the color of the hair are words that describe each woman's temperament. Blondes are sweet and devoted, black-haired women are ardent, redheads are coquettish and full of tricks, while brunettes are discreet and sincere.

"Brunettes are dull," Nise says. "Discreet and sincere."

"Well, redheads are troublemakers," I say.

"I don't know," he says, smiling a little. "I think there's some truth to it all."

"How could there be any truth to it?" I say.

"If I slept with you, you would exhaust me," he tells me. Then he turns to Nise and says, "I think you would renew me."

After he says it, I know he is watching, studying our faces for our reactions. But I keep mine as blank as I can.

"It's just what I think," he says.

I know he must be trying to shock or agitate us, but nothing changes in his expression, and then I know he is serious, or half-serious. Which is ridiculous. Not because he said something outright about sleeping with the two of us, but because he thinks he has some idea what it would be like to be with either one of us.

"So the two of you would exhaust each other, and I would be left to pick up the pieces," Nise says then, shaking her head. "No thank you."

We laugh, even he laughs, and that quickly, in an instant, everything becomes teasing again.

But even though Nise has made his words a teasing thing, it

is clear he is willing to say anything to us. And I know I am right about him. It all may be a fantasy or a game to him, but he is intent upon the game. Intent upon us.

The three of us go back to paging through *Journal Pour Tous*, chatting idly, but in a little while he tells us he has to go and meet a friend. That he really just stopped by Baudon to see if he could catch us.

"My working girls," he says. "You have a demanding schedule."

"What friend?" Nise wants to know.

"Antonin. Tonin is what I call him."

"D'accord," she says. "I just wanted to see if you had a name ready."

He shakes his head and kisses my cheek, and then kisses Nise's cheek. Before he goes, he leaves money on the table. It is more than enough to pay for our wine. Enough to pay for our wine and buy us dinner.

After he leaves, Nise says to me, "What was that about, really?"

"He wanted to tell us what he thought it would be like to sleep with us."

I look over at the couple at the table closest to ours. They are playing dominoes and do not look up, but I know they heard everything that has been said. I do not care. I am seventeen and neither my mother's rules nor my father's love could change me. I do not care what anyone thinks of me except for Nise.

I do not know it yet, but that is something else he is giving me. Even with my dirty hair and in my filthy work dress, there is something in me that sets me apart. I thought it was the green boots of a whore and the way Nise and I look when we stand drawing, like we are some kind of picture ourselves, but now I see it is not just that. It is something else altogether and it does not have anything to do with a pair of boots or anything I can slip on.

It has to do with me.

After le maître brings the bowls, we sit in our damp work dresses and eat our beef stew. Listen to the sound of the dominoes clicking down.

he day we met him, Nise told him she had never been anywhere, but it is a lie. She goes back home to Toucy every couple of months. There was no reason to tell him anything that day when we were just making conversation, and maybe it does not count because Toucy is her home. In any case it is her business and her business alone.

I went along once. Because I was curious but also to keep her company. Because I knew it busted her up to go. It always does. She always says she should go, and yet she dreads to go. But if she puts it off too long, she feels miserable.

Her parents raise the girl as if she were Nise's sister. And in a way she is: Nise had her when she was fifteen.

Sometimes I want to ask her what it was like to have a baby. I think she would tell me, but I do not ask. The day I went with her, she was quiet most of the day and got happier the farther away we got from Toucy. Or maybe that is putting it too strongly. Maybe she just seemed relieved. Glad it was over but also glad she had gone. Glad the duty was over for another couple of months, which would mean a couple of months she would not have to think of what she should do.

"Do you miss her?" I asked on the train back that day.

"I don't know her."

I nodded and she looked at me and smiled a little, but then she looked away. She did not say anything else for a long time, and after that, I noticed how her eyes were puffier. It was not from crying—I would have heard that. I mean it just tired her to go. The skin under her eyes stayed puffy for the whole next day, and her faraway eye looked especially tired.

The thing is, nothing about Nise makes you think she has a kid. She is always going on about how she is more practical than I am, and she is. But there is a kind of sweetness about her that seems so real and is so real, even when she is being tough and cursing in her funny, husking voice. It does not seem to fit with what she had to go through. Or maybe it does fit. Maybe it is the sweetness and the goodness in her that makes her able to be the way she is in spite of everything.

And maybe that is the thing he sees. Her kindness. Maybe it is why he said that stupidity about how she would renew him after I exhausted him. Or maybe he thinks she is innocent altogether. For one thing, she does not look nineteen, and there is always that dream men have, that someone is innocent under her skirts. As if anyone ever were innocent, or innocent for very long.

Anyway, that is how she comes home today. Tired from the

trip. Eyes puffy. Quiet. She tells me something about the train ride, but that is all. It will take her a couple of days to get back to herself.

Aimée. That is the little girl's name. She looks a little like Nise but mostly not.

This time we meet him outside a brasserie, Flicoteaux's.

We all go inside together, and when we get to a corner table he stands aside so I can take a seat along the wall, on the banquette. He goes on standing and waiting, and I assume that Nise will slip in beside me, that we will both sit across from him, which is how we sat both other times. He takes the duty of feeding us seriously, and I think he likes being able to watch us stuff ourselves.

But Nise does not do what I expect her to do, or what he expects her to do. She takes the chair opposite me.

Maybe she just wanted to give him the more comfortable seat on the banquette because it is where you can see the rest of the room instead of turning your back to it. But whether it is on purpose or not, she makes him choose who to sit beside, her or me. Brunette or redhead.

And in a second he does decide. In a second he is sliding next to me, and Nise is on the other side of the table. If she feels anything she does not show it, at least not that I can see. But maybe I am not looking hard enough.

We are not there long before a man comes over and stands beside the table and begins to talk. The man looks like a student, only older, and it is clear the man is some kind of friend of his, or at least an acquaintance. Though he does not invite the man to join us, he willingly talks to him.

"So things are fine in your mind, then?" the man asks. "The coup succeeds and there's nothing more to it?"

"People got tired," he says. "They got tired of mobs in the streets. They wanted something to happen and it did. Louis-Napoléon happened."

"And now everyone's content to be shipmates of a pirate, as Hugo says."

"Not content. But they accept."

"But how can that be?" the man asks. "You were there at the Sallandrouze. You saw the carnage."

"I was there," he tells the man. "Even so."

And everything changes at that moment. I know then that he does not want to go on talking to the man because his words have become clipped, precise. But the man does not hear it.

"How can anyone align with that?" the man says, and for the first time I really see the wildness in the man's eyes. He is dressed like a student but he is too old to be a student, and there is something off about him, something haggard.

"It's not a question of alignment," he tells the man, and his voice is even quieter than before. "It's just living day to day."

"I'm surprised that you would say that. Above all people."

He laughs a little. "Don't be surprised, Legrand," he says. "I'm no better than the next man."

I go on listening for a while, I do, but then I let the words become sounds. Sometimes when he is listening to the haggard man speak, he leans my way a little, and I feel the hardness of his shoulder against mine. Or when he picks up his glass of wine, sometimes his arm bumps against me. But I never move away—I want to feel him against me.

And in a little while, whether from the sitting close or just the wine we are drinking, I want to feel more than just occasional bumps against my shoulder and elbow. Maybe I want him to turn his attention back to us and away from the man. But as soon as I think it, I know even that is not truth.

I want him to turn his attention to me.

He has kept things fair between Nise and me and maybe I should, too, but he chose me to sit beside and it is my side he keeps touching tonight, and I want him to know my feelings.

So I make him pay attention to me.

I pivot—that is the only way to say it—I pivot my arm at the elbow, turning it so my shoulder does not move, so only my forearm moves, there underneath the table. And I slip my hand over his leg. A secret touch that I tell myself Nise will not see, nor the man who is standing there, talking and talking.

He is mid-sentence in something, still talking to the tattered man, and he does not turn his head my way or break his speaking in any way, but he immediately takes my hand in his. Squeezes my hand hard in his and then holds my hand against his thigh. And then it does not matter that I kept my shoulder still because my whole arm moves in tandem with his, and it becomes perfectly clear what I have done.

Nise sees it. Something bright flashes in her eyes and then she shifts in her chair and looks away. And I tell myself she should not care, because even if he had taken the chair beside her, she would not have dared to pivot her arm and touch him. I know that. If he chose to sit beside her, it would have all been wasted on her.

But it is not wasted on me.

Because there is nowhere else to look, Nise stares up at the man who is too old to be a student, who is still standing beside the table. And the man sees her watching him, sees the brightness in her eyes, and decides she has a genuine interest in the conversation. So he says to Nise, "What do you think, then, of our leader, mademoiselle?"

"I think no matter what the emperor does, I still have to go to work tomorrow," she tells him. "That's what I think."

There is not much the too-old student can say to that, and I want to laugh at how dismayed he looks by her words. But she is right. Because whatever else is true, it is she and I who go to work each day. Not the one who looks like a ragged student, and certainly not him, even if he does put on a shabby coat when he comes to see us.

The man turns away after that. It finally seems to dawn on

him that he has been intruding on an intimate dinner, and he looks for a way to exit. To leave us all to our own devices.

After the man walks away—leaves or goes to stand next to someone else's table—I say, "What's Sallandrouze? What were you talking about?"

"The Hôtel Sallandrouze," he says. "It's just a place."

"Did something happen there?"

"Something happened there and I saw it."

"What was it?"

He rubs his fingers over my hand for a long time before he answers. Keeps going back to the calluses.

Looking at neither of us, he says, "It happened a long time ago. And I saw what everyone else saw that day. Soldiers and shooting."

Both Nise and I are quiet, but in a moment she says, "It sounds terrible. I don't think I want to hear about it."

"I don't want to tell you about it," he says. "And it's foolish to talk about it, even here. Legrand should know that."

So I do not say that I want to hear. That I want to know. I want to know because I know it matters to him. I can feel that it matters in his hand and along his leg.

"Let's talk about more pleasant things," he says to us then. "What's the gossip on the floor of Baudon?"

But neither Nise nor I volunteer anything, and in another moment he says, "It seems we've run out of things to say. It seems you're both my silent wives."

Maybe we have all of us run out of things to say, or maybe it is just the quiet after all the political talk. But of course I know it is something else: Nise is quiet because she knows I am touching him, still, and it is usually she who keeps the conversation going.

I am about to say something—anything—but just then the waiter brings our food.

Only then does he give me back my hand. So I can use my knife and fork. So I can use my hand to eat.

❧

After we finish dinner, he reaches across the table and takes Nise's hand and then he takes my hand again. He studies Nise's fingers, whose nails are cut down almost to the quick, and mine that have a sliver of white on each nail. But both our hands are red, and I am sure he is right about our calluses. They probably are in the same spots on our palms and fingers.

"I want to sleep with both of you," he tells us.

That is all. No more comments about who would exhaust him and who would replenish him. He says only what is necessary.

Nise looks at me and then at him. "Both of us together," she says. "That's what you mean, isn't it? That she and I share you."

"We share each other," he says. "All of us together, as we are now."

Nise waits, so I wait, too. I know she will say something, and I want to hear it. I want to hear it before I say anything.

"Oh, I don't know," she says. "What if I don't want to share my toys?"

He looks at her after she says it, after she tries to turn his words into a joke. She does not say anything else, though, and when he looks at me, I do not say a word. Because I am the silent wife? Because I cannot say now what I would have said before?

"It's the only thing I think of," he tells us then. "Not politics, not history. Just the two of you." And he goes on holding her hand and mine. Watching us.

Even though Nise just said she did not want to share, at that moment she is. She does not pull her hand away, so she is sharing him with me, and sharing me with him. All of us are connected whether she wants it or not.

But I do not say that. Because I think words are just sounds anyway.

~✥~

That night when he walks us home, he turns at Rue Jacinthe, which is a street that is more like a passageway or an alley than a street. He stops at the first doorway down from the wine shop. When I see what he wants, when he stops and turns toward Nise, I let go of the crook of his arm. Before I walk away, though, I see his arms go up around Nise's waist. I watch that much and then I walk back down to the window of the wine shop and wait.

I wait a little while, thinking of Nise and him, and then I wait longer, thinking of everything he said at Flicoteaux's. Not just what he said to Nise and me—I think of what he talked about with the man who was too old to be a student. I think about the way his face looked when he said, "Soldiers and shooting." At first I didn't think those words fit in with the rest of the night—with touching him under the table, or with him telling us he wants to sleep with both of us. But now I think the words do fit. The words fit because they happened. Time is never just one way, and nothing is ever just one thing. Things always blend together.

I do not know how long I wait, but when I hear Nise's footsteps come toward me, I hardly glance at her. I walk in the direction she came from, down to the darkened doorway.

He is waiting there, leaning in the entryway, one shoulder against the frame of the door. And then I am not thinking about soldiers or the ragged man or how things get blended together.

"You look like a real type," I tell him. "Un maquereau. Just waiting for his girl."

I want to be the one to talk this time. To tease him. To show him that I am not always silent. That I am there not because he chose me but because I choose to be.

He takes me by my hands and I think he will kiss me then because I saw him kiss Nise. But he does not kiss me, not right away. Instead he holds my hands and moves them down so they are against the front of his coat, the front of his trousers. When I do not stop him, he moves them all the way down. So I can feel him. He keeps his eyes on mine, and even in the dim light I can see him watching my face as I touch him through cloth.

But I am studying him, too. The long hair that waves back. How his face looks so bruised and open.

"You aren't afraid, are you?" he asks, and his voice sounds bruised, too. "You're never afraid."

So I say, "I'm never afraid."

I say it because he wants me to but also because it is true. I am seventeen and I am not afraid of anything yet.

He kisses me. I keep one hand pressed against him, fingers down. I put the other hand up by his mouth so I can feel the kiss that way, too, the same way I did with my soldier.

What I can feel is he is hungry the way Nise and I are hungry when we sit down at a table with him. I am seventeen and at that moment I understand that when a man is hungry like that, what he really needs is to have something taken from him.

So I take his tongue on mine. Like fruit, like chocolate.

Like salt.

That *night after Nise and* I go to bed, I wait until we are both lying in the darkness. I want to ask her if she touched him the way I did, if he held her hands to him the way he held mine.

But I already know it was something he did with me alone. Because I pivoted my arm, because I slipped my hand over his leg at the restaurant, because I am the one who would exhaust him.

Because Nise is different. He assigned her a different personality, a different role in the game.

So instead I ask, "Do you want to stop?"

"Do you?"

"No."

"Then why ask?"

"Because we can," I say. "We can stop." Yet even as I say the words I am not sure I mean them. I am not sure I can stop.

What I do know is she is my family, not him. Ma frangine.

And then, almost as if she can read my thoughts, I feel her do what she sometimes does: she reaches across the bed and wraps her hand in my hair for a moment. Gives it a gentle tug.

"I think we would have stopped already if we wanted to," she says, and uncoils her hand.

"Do you still think he's harmless?"

"No."

"What is he then?" I say.

"Something."

I think she might say something else but she does not, and neither do I. If he kissed her differently than he kissed me, I do not want to know. Because even though he has tried to keep things equal, they cannot be, and she and I both know that. Or maybe I know it especially. It would seem I would have the advantage tonight because I am the one who touched him under the table, because it was my hands he held up against him, but it will hurt me if Nise tells me he said something sweet to her when they kissed. Because maybe she gets the sweetness and I get the hunger.

I lie awake thinking of the way the cloth of his trousers felt, and how his cock felt through the cloth. I think about how the last man I touched was my soldier, the one I walked with until I liked him well enough to kiss, the one who held me on the cushion of his thighs. I think about all those things until I hear Nise's breathing change. It is a little rasping sound, the tiniest scraping.

Like a fingernail against cloth.

walk down Rue Jacinthe the next day.

The street is one building long, connecting Rue Galande and Rue des Trois-Portes. If you stand in the middle of it, you can almost touch the buildings on either side.

I go to the door where he and I stood and touched. And wonder if the wood remembers me.

M en see us and the idea comes to them. A brunette and a redhead, the two of us together, the novelty of it.

And they all think it is original.

It is why Moulin wanted us, it is why he paid us to come to his studio for photographs. Silver gelatins, he called them. And it is why we took the money. Because we could do it together. I was still apprenticing at Baudon for nothing, and I did not want to run home to my parents. I thought, *If we go there together it will not be so bad. If I go with Nise it will not be hard.*

The place is at Rue Richer 23. That is the address Moulin gives. But the studio itself is on Rue du Faubourg Montmartre, up in the attic. Parts of the roof have been replaced with glass, but then he changes the light coming through the panes by sliding strips of fabric across them. He tilts a big cheval mirror to focus that cloth-filtered light.

Depending on the pose, we could see ourselves in that mirror. He told us he wanted pictures of us together. That was what he paid for, and that was what he really wanted. But those poses were hardest. Nise on the divan and me standing beside, brushing her hair. A stupid stance with my head on Nise's breast and a string of fake pearls around us. Both of us on the lace-covered divan, her with her back to Moulin, looking over her shoulder, and me with my head on her shoulder, facing straight on, legs parted.

All of it made me sweat in my armpits and at the nape of my neck, even though I was not really doing anything.

It was not just hard to be naked, but the poses felt fake. If he had been able to show Nise and me the way we are sometimes— one of us standing at the basin in our room, soaping herself, and the other lying on the bed. One of us playing with herself, stroking the hair between her legs, while the other talks aimlessly. The lazy, idle touching we do when we are waiting for the other to come to bed or to wake up. Even me standing and plucking the one red hair from my nipple while Nise gets dressed. Those things would have felt normal. Natural. What Moulin asked did not feel like that, but how could it in a studio where the light is shining and everything has to take place on a divan? How could it be normal in front of a stranger?

At the end he took pictures of each of us alone. That went better. I could see what he was after. Could see the beauty in it.

My favorite pose of Nise was her just standing there, her head tilted, holding her chemise loose in her hand, her arm down by her side. Not that I saw the picture itself, but from what I saw of the pose. Her face looked so sweet and shy. Her head was tilted to the side, and she looked as if she really might just be standing there in our room, talking to me about something that happened at work or something we saw on the street. Talking about anything. She did not look her age—she looked about fourteen. Moulin saw it, too. I know he did. He did not say anything but I could feel it in the way he looked at her.

Moulin said she looked *farouche.* I thought only an animal could be that way, but that is how he thought Nise looked. Savagely shy. I could see it once he said it. To me she just looked like Nise.

It was hard to say which of my poses were best because I could not see them all in the cheval glass. I think maybe one where I was lying on my side, up on one elbow, my back to Moulin and his camera. The indentation at my waist, the cleft my bottom knee made under the other—even I could see it was pretty when I glanced back in the mirror. Hair smoothed back from my warm face but down on my shoulders.

The thing about redheads is we do not really have eyebrows. That is how my face looked in the cheval glass, at least to me.

When we got out of Moulin's studio, the first thing Nise said was, "The bottoms of your feet were filthy."

"Yours too."

We laughed about it. Maybe out of embarrassment, maybe out of relief. Maybe out of happiness over the money. Twenty francs for each of us.

"Would you go back?" I say.

"Never."

"If we needed money?"

"You're almost done apprenticing," Nise said. "You'll get paid a real wage soon."

"But don't you think it got easier the longer we were there?"

"It just seemed that way," she said.

And I understood then that the whole thing had been different for her somehow. Because at some point when I was lying there on Moulin's throw, I began to pretend. I know I did. I began to pretend that the thing he was asking me to do was no different from a thing I wanted to do myself. The thing Moulin wanted from me became a thing I wanted, and the way he wanted to see me—with the cheval mirror reflecting the filmy light from the roof and my hair spilling down over my shoulders—became a new way I wanted to see myself.

It became a bit like the way I feel each time I put on my green boots. They are just boots but they change the whole way I see myself. Because of their color, because they were a gift from a whore, because they signify something entirely different from shoes my mother and father gave me. Something.

Moulin wrote our names down. The made-up names we told him at first, as well as our real ones. *Mlles Louise Meurent 16 ans (dite l'Arc-en-ciel) et son amie Pâquerette (Denise Desroziers) 18 ans.* That is who we were for Moulin, Rainbow and Daisy. Somewhere in his studio it is written down.

ot the next day but the day after he shows up outside Baudon.

This time I half expect it. But I should not say it like that, because while it does not surprise me to see him standing there, waiting for us, the sight of him is still a surprise to me. The waving hair, the loose way he stands, smoking in the street. The mustache that I now know hides crooked front teeth—I know because I felt them with my tongue.

His details surprise me.

Or maybe I am just happy to see him standing there.

Today I do not feel embarrassed by my filthy dress, I just take his arm and so does Nise. It is easier than it was the other day. He could be other places but instead he is there, waiting for us.

"What way do you take home from work?" he asks.

"It's nothing special," Nise says.

"All the same," he says. "Montrez-moi."

So we fall into walking in our style, three abreast, and we show him what we can: the clock place and the porcelain workshop around the corner from Baudon; all the clothing hanging under the sign of Le Goût du Jour (with dresses in every color from garish to drab); Pincemail Tourneur sur Boix et Métaux, where the workers wear caps and blouses; F. Descamps, with its three rows of men's boots hanging on rods to the left of the door and three rows of women's boots hanging on rods to the right of the door; the place on Rue des Marmousets where you almost always see carts but sometimes a horse waiting patiently, too, with checkered sacks in his cart; the orange and white cat at the beurre et oeuf shop on the quai; and lastly the place where we buy apple fritters to eat when we get near home. He buys six, two for each of us.

"Now the room," he says. "Let's see where the tour ends."

"Why are you so interested?" Nise asks him, and I know she is thinking of whatever mess we left that day: dirty wash water from the morning, our night things. Though in truth the place is never really in disarray because we do not own enough to leave in disarray.

"I thought you were the one who invited me the other night," he says.

"That was before."

"Before what?"

And I see the corner she has backed herself into. She invited him the other night knowing he would say no, as I did. We invited him to tease him only.

"Before she knew we'd be friends," I tell him, and then I turn to her. "Let him see it, Nise," I say. "Since he wants to."

So we go up. He trails us up the five flights and then steps into our hole. But he does not pause on the doorstep, does not peer around carefully, examining or judging. Instead he follows us right in, takes the single seat on the spidery chair we offer him while we sit on the bed, so that the three of us can eat the apple fritters, still warm, from their papers.

Still, I look around the room to try to see it as he does. There are the smudged walls and the broken sconce beside the door. My green boots stand by my side of the bed, and our two better dresses hang on nails on the back of the door. The basin on the old dresser whose one leg is broken and propped up on a tin. Our washrags. A tiny china bird Nise brought from Toucy that she keeps on the table, along with the cheap carnets and pencils we cart around. Not much to see.

So we eat. And do not talk. Nise and I do not even pretend to be polite about the fritters. We just fall on them, eating them as quickly as we can, as quickly as we want for once, not trying to parcel out a single one to make it last.

"Really," Nise says when we are done, when she is wiping her greasy fingers and mouth on her washrag. "Why did you want to come here?"

"I wanted to see where you live. Where you wash your faces," he says, and nods once at the rag in her hand.

He is sitting at the deal table, where he has been going through my sketchbook. There is nothing new in it since the day we met him and I drew the glob of a cat asleep behind the window with *Repassage Tous les Jours*, so he looks at the old drawings. The horse that pulls the cart loaded with checkered sacks. Different buildings. More cats in windows. Flowers from the day I went to Toucy with Nise. Her mother had morning glories growing up some strings outside her kitchen window, and I drew them while Nise talked to her mother and played with Aimée.

"Does that mean you're going to show us where you live?" Nise asks him.

"I see you like animals," he tells me. "Animals and flowers." Then he turns to Nise and says, "I'll show you by and by."

She makes a sound in her throat but does not say anything. I do not know if she feels caught out again, the way she felt the first time he showed up at our work, or if she feels he is trying to trick us. Maybe it is my pictures of her mother's flowers and thoughts of Toucy that upset her.

"Can I sit there with both of you?"

He asks us both but I know he mostly means the question for Nise. He does not want her to be upset so he directs his attention to her, and when he comes to sit between us on the bed, she is the one he holds first.

I do not look away. I want to watch him kiss her. And in a moment or two I see he is not the same with her as he is with me. It is a different kiss he gives her and takes from her.

I know I cannot feel the kiss, but there is something quieter about the way he explores her mouth. I sense the same deliberateness, the same hunger that I feel with him, but still the kiss is different.

Or maybe he is not different at all, maybe this is just what it is to kiss Nise. And maybe she is conscious of me watching, and maybe I am the one changing the kiss.

It is all so close I cannot tell.

When I think that I get up. I stand up—so I can walk away, so she can kiss him the way she wants. But when I start to step away, he catches at my hand and pulls me back. Toward him and her and our bed and that careful, thoughtful kiss. And he keeps my hand in his as he kisses her, as he touches her hair and throat and jaw with his other hand.

Whatever it means to him, whatever it makes him feel to keep my hand in his as he kisses her, I do not know because I stop watching. I stand there but I close my eyes, and in that way I give her privacy. I give her what privacy I can as he keeps me close to their kiss. I do not have to give him privacy—he does not want it.

With my eyes closed I cannot see my green boots or Nise's china bird or our sketchpads on the table or the basin or the blue box of candles with *Éviter les contrefaçons.* Can only hear.

When it is my turn—when the sound of the kiss stops and he gently shakes me by my hand and pulls me toward him—my mind feels blank. Erased. But then I feel something else. Foolish about being kept beside him so long, annoyed by keeping my eyes closed in my own room. So I stand between his legs and I pull his hair back from his face. I keep my fingers tight in his hair and when I kiss him, I run my tongue as hard as I can over his teeth. I do not want him to confuse my kiss or my mouth or my taste with hers.

My impatience comes through in the kiss, and I want to be sure he feels it. There are things I want, too.

We know his age now—thirty—and though he is not as old as we thought when we first met him, it is still true that he is closer in age to my father than me. Still, in his fawn-colored pants and special vests, even in today's worn coat, he is nothing like my father. As people say, he is from a different rung of the ladder.

I think what it must be like for him to be there with us, two girls on a narrow bed, two girls in their work dresses, two girls who are not from his world.

But because we are not from his world, he can be anything he wants here with us. And however exotic he is to us, that is exactly how exotic we are to him. It is why he is stretched out on our quilt, talking as idly with us as Nise and I talk to each other. It is why he can say anything he wants to us.

"Just the thought of the two of you sleeping in this bed," he says now, and shakes his head. "Now I'll have the right place to picture it."

"So that's why you wanted to come here," Nise says.

I do not say anything. It all makes sense now that he has said it. It is not the particulars of the room or even our poorness that he came to see. He just wanted to spy on us a little. Except it is not spying because he is right there with us. Picturing us and telling us about it.

Now he points to me with his chin. "The redhead can take it," he says.

The comment is not tied to anything, and I think he will follow it with something about Nise because that is what he always does. I am the silent wife and she is the talkative one, I would exhaust him and she would renew him. But he does not say anything else. He just lies there on the bed with us.

What can I take, I want to ask. A joke? A cock? Or maybe just the idea of him wanting to sleep with the two of us.

Whatever it is he means, the words sound lewd to me. I know I am lying there on my bed with him and Nise, but his words still surprise me. Still shock me. *The redhead can take it.*

Nise does not say anything and does not meet my eyes. And because I cannot see her eyes, I cannot know what she is thinking. But something in the way she lies there, silently, makes me wonder if she is not somehow pleased that he said the crude thing to me. Not to her. Never to her.

I do know that whatever it is he has decided about me, it is something he has not decided about Nise. With her gentleness and her ability to renew.

That is what I see in the plum shadows beneath his eyes.

That night after he leaves, before we go to sleep, I see Nise has gotten her period. When she undresses, I can see her fiddling with the rag, even though she turns away.

Which means I'll get mine soon. First her, then me, or the other way around—we bleed at the same time.

"Are you ready for the light?" she says when she is done.

"I'm ready."

So she blows out the candle. We had to start a new box tonight. We are out of La Favorite and on to a red box of Rat de Cave.

We do not talk about him.

Before she crawls into bed, when she is pulling on her oldest chemise, I see her backbone. The bones look like pebbles. Like a line of pebbles.

There was a time when I was getting to know Nise that things were different between us. At least they were for me.

I had just moved into the room with her on Maître-Albert. I left my parents so I could do as I pleased, but things had ended with the man I liked and I was heartsick.

Nise knew it. She tried to be kind to me. I was sitting at the table with my head down on my arms and she came over and hugged my shoulders.

"I'll braid your hair for you," she said. "Didn't you always like it when your mother did that for you?"

So she brushed my hair and played with it and finally made a crown of braids in it. At first when she was brushing my hair, I was still talking about the man. But then I stopped. It made my head feel so drowsy and good to have her fingers in my hair. Her hands felt like little birds at my temples, at my nape.

If she had leaned over and kissed my neck or reached forward and touched my breasts, I would have understood. That is how loving it all felt. And in a little while I wished she would touch me that way.

I tried to tell her. I did not say the words but I tried to tell her through my skin. Which probably just sounds stupid. But I tried to let her know how I felt. I tried to tell her through my skin that she could touch me more. That I wanted her to touch me. Like a lover.

But she did not touch me except to finish the braids and hug me again.

"You'll feel better soon," she said. "You'll see."

I did feel better soon. New things happened and I forgot about the man who caused so much heartache.

Men touching your sex, your breasts, wanting to bend you backwards with their embraces—it is easy to get those things. But someone's hands in your hair so softly they feel like small birds—that confused me.

For a little while I thought I was in love with her, but then I understood. It was the touching I wanted. I did not really want her, I just wanted it done.

A sign on the corner of Rue Descartes and Rue Clovis:

MAISON D'ÉDUCATION DE DEMOISELLES
RUE DU POT DE FER 7
GRAND JARDIN POUR LA RÉCRÉATION

I wonder, where did I get my education?

From my parents. From the whores my mother sewed for. At Baudon.

And the streets can be a garden, in a manner of speaking.

That he is not what he said he was goes without saying. That he was more than what he claimed—we understood that. Not a tax collector, which he already admitted, and also not Eugène and not from Gennevilliers, which we guessed. Still, we do not know the whole colossal extent of it until he takes us there to Rue Guyot. The studio itself is nothing—a shabby building, surrounded by depots. But it is filled with paintings, some framed, some not. Some hang but most just lean against the walls.

What does not make sense is why someone like him would want to lie. I know why Nise and I lie. But why lie if you already are something in the world?

We look and look. Of course I like the small, funny sketches of cats—he showed them to us first.

"Why didn't you just laugh at me the day you saw me drawing?" I say when I see one watercolor of a calico. "What a joke it must have been."

"Why would I laugh? You saw something and wanted to draw it."

But it must have been a joke to him. Part of the game.

As we look around we cannot help but notice the area he has set up by the windows. It is its own little room within the room, and it could just be a place to sit or rest but it isn't. For one thing the blue divan is out away from the wall, on display in the room, and a big cheval glass is positioned so it reflects the light from the windows onto the divan. When I see it I smile and shake my head a little.

"What does that remind you of?" I say to Nise.

"I know."

When he looks at us, I know I should not say anything, but I do. "Another studio," I tell him.

"Whose?"

"A place on Rue Richer."

"You mean Félix's? Do you know him then?"

"We don't know him," Nise says. "We went there once."

"Did he take pictures of you?"

"The two of us," I say.

He goes to a cabinet then and pulls out some cards. Brings them to a table by the window to show us.

"These came from Félix Moulin."

One card shows a sullen young girl. She is looking off away from the camera, but even so I can see her expression, her flat eyes. You can just make out the side of her breast.

The second photo is as different from the first as it can be.

It shows a bare-breasted young woman seated sideways on a chair, her arm bent, resting her head against her hand. Her skirts are pulled up and you can see the sides of her legs, the top crossed over the bottom, the bottom knee pointing forward a little. She still has her white stockings on, and her garters buckle just above her knees. There is a dark shadow between her legs where her sex is, the smallest of spaces peeking out from beneath her top thigh, but because of the way she is sitting, her sex is hidden.

Nothing shows between her legs, but you look—you have to look because that is what the picture is about.

That small shadow of her sex.

In spite of the shadow, it is the woman's face I cannot stop looking at. Someone has made her cheeks red, along with her lips and necklace and a stripe in her skirt. They put the red toward the front of her cheeks, as if she were blushing. But when I look at her face—the face underneath the painted-on blush—I can see the real her. Instead of rosy and merry, the way someone wanted to show her, she looks serious. Tired. Maybe a little sad. It is hard to say because she is looking off to the left and people always look a little sad when you see their glance fall somewhere else. When you catch them thinking, being quiet in themselves.

He sees me studying the photo and tells me, "She was popular a few years ago. Augustine."

"Elle est jolie," I say. "Prettier than the other one. The other one looks bored."

"You think that's what it is? That she's bored?"

"I don't know," I say. I do not want to say that the girl's eyes look dead to me. That what I see in her goes far beyond bored. "It's hard to tell from a picture."

"I have others," he says.

But instead of showing more, he puts the photos away. Only then do I realize that Nise has not been studying the photos as I have. That she has wandered across the studio to where a window looks out on a shabby courtyard. He does not want to lose her entirely so he puts his photographs away.

I would have gone on looking.

⤙⤚

When the three of us sit down on the divan I think it is good it does not have a lace throw. If it did I think I would start to laugh again, or Nise would—something. When we first sit down, he holds one of each of our hands but then he lets go. Lies back and crosses his arms behind his head so he can look at us.

"What was it like? To pose?"

"I got overheated," I said.

"Did you?"

"You don't do things like that in real life," I say. "We don't sit around holding a string of pearls between us. Pillowing our heads on each other."

"No, I imagine not," he says. Then, because Nise has not said anything, he turns to her and asks, "What did you think of it?"

"I wouldn't do it again."

"Not ever?" he asks.

"Never."

When she says that, she looks off at the light coming in the windows. He sits up again, there between us. I think he is going to say something else but he does not. He takes Nise's hand in his again and moves his head close to her shoulder.

So I say, "You kissed her first last time. In our room."

Which is selfish. I know she wishes I did not tell him anything about posing for Moulin, I know she is feeling whatever she feels. But I take the hand of his closest to me and move it up to my breast.

"Kiss me first this time," I tell him.

So he does. He kisses me first. I feel both of his arms go round me and that is how I know he has let go of Nise's hand.

I know she is sitting there beside us, but I do not let myself think about it. I do not think about anything but getting him to touch me.

꒰ꞏ꒱

When we are done kissing—when everyone has had their turn—Nise says to him, "So that's what you wanted that first day."

"What did I want?"

She gestures around us. "To put us in your pictures."

"I couldn't paint the two of you," he says.

"Why?"

"If I painted like Botticelli I couldn't paint you." And when he sees the name means nothing to us, he says, "He painted angels. Red-haired and brown-haired and blonde angels."

"Why can't you paint us like yourself?"

"I couldn't paint you as you are. To paint you as you are, I'd have to paint this," he says, and leans down and kisses my breast through my dress. When he goes to touch Nise, though, she stands up.

"Are you tired of it already?" he says.

She shakes her head no, but then she says, "Maybe. It's all a game to you. The two of us."

She is right. We are a game to him. But he is serious about the game, and what he wants is for none of us to tire of it. For all three of us to go on teasing and kissing and touching. All of us blending together. I think that is why he says the next thing.

"If I slept with just one of you, I would ruin your friendship," he tells us.

I know he partly says it to see our reaction, to see the effect of his words. And for a moment there is an effect. I want to strike out at him for thinking he knows anything about us. But instead I watch him, just the way he watches me, and what I see is this: now that he has said the thing, he seems mournful. As if he were imagining the future he just foretold, or weighing the choice in front of him. Brunette or redhead. He looks sorrowful at the thought of losing either one of us. Just a little while ago he was touching our breasts through our dresses, and even now his arm is still around my back.

"Why would you say that?" Nise asks. "She and I are sisters."

"Oh, I see that," he says. "I see that clearly."

"Sisters, not lovers."

When she says that I think it must be what is really wrong. It is not the sharing that bothers her, at least not the taking turns. It is the idea of the three of us together. The same fantasy that

Moulin had. With his silly poses and the string of fake pearls, Moulin wanted Nise and me to play at being lovers. But we were not lovers. Not even the night she had her hands in my hair, when I wanted her to touch me. When I wanted to touch her.

I could echo her words about being sisters right now, I could echo her impatience—but I do not. Because I would sleep with him and with her. With my frangine. I would share him, but I would share her, too.

And at that moment, in his studio, I know things are changing. I know each one of us is deciding something.

What I do not know is that his words are a kind of slow poison, and that they have already started to do their damage.

꘎

It begins that night after he walks us home, when he says goodnight to us.

We have spent the day kissing, so when he says goodnight he kisses each of us quickly. We do not linger and he does not pull either of us into a doorway—none of that. He tells us he is going to walk over to La Maube to see if he can get a carriage, and we part.

Nise and I are almost to the door of our building when I tell her, "I can't. I don't want to go in. I want to go to him."

We look at each other for just a second but then I turn away. I look away from Nise, back down Maître-Albert to see if I can still see him. I do not see her face when she says, "Go then."

I do not see her face—all I hear are the two words. I do not take time to see the feeling in her face.

I run down the street, looking ahead, but I cannot see around the corner, and he must be moving quickly, much more quickly than he did when he had one of us on each arm.

For a second before I catch up to him, he is just a man, a stranger on the street, and then I am standing beside him, touching him on the arm.

"Trine," he says.

He is surprised to see me, I can tell that, but I can tell from his voice he is also pleased. And in that moment I realize that I have been counting on his pleasure. That I would not have known what to do if he were not pleased.

But because he said my name and because he is glad to see me, I can say the next thing.

"That wasn't a real kiss," I say. "I don't want to say goodnight without a real kiss."

He looks at me then, and I do not read the expression on his face as much as I feel it. It is not the pleasant expression he sometimes puts on when he is with the two of us—it is something raw. But I do not get to look at his face for long because he pulls me toward him, and then he is wrapping about me.

The kiss is real. Not an exploration of my mouth, not a game on a divan. A man's kiss, as if we were going to lie down together. And when the kiss is done, when we both pull back to look at each other, he still keeps his arms around me.

"Is that better?"

When I nod yes, he says, "You should go back. Denise will be worried about you."

"She knows where I am."

"Still, she'll worry."

He walks me back almost to the dogleg of the street. When I look to the entrance of our building, I think I might see Nise standing there, but of course she is not there. Of course she has gone inside.

He kisses me again, lightly, but this time I accept it. I accept it and walk up to 17 and go inside.

When I get to our room, Nise is there in her oldest chemise, the one she sleeps in. Scrubbing her face.

"I watched for you for a while. Until you turned the corner," she says. "So you caught up to him?"

"He was on La Maube."

"Did you kiss him?"

"Yes," I say.

"I hoped you kissed him for me, too."

I nod then but do not say anything. There is nothing to say. Nise could have come. Could have turned and run with me, back down the street. But she did not, and I know that, somewhere in my mind, I have already taken his words to heart.

He will sleep with one of us, and it will be me.

He chose me the night he ate cherries from my hand, he chose me the night he sat beside me in the restaurant, he chose me when he held my hand over him, so I could feel his cock.

He has said he wants us both. Yet each time he has a choice, he chooses me.

By the time I crawl into bed beside Nise, there is a tiny wall between us that was not there before.

But things can be like that. You can be so close with a person and still not tell them everything. You can choose not to say something, you can withhold something, you can lie to someone you love. I have known that since I was a child.

So maybe his words were not poison at all. Maybe it was in me all along.

t turns out to be the easiest thing.

It is Sunday, and we sleep in a little. But when we do wake up, the words are ready in my mind to say. I do not have to think them—they are there, ready when I need them.

"I'm going to go see my mother," I tell Nise. "I want her to help me with that dress."

And as I am saying it, I am picturing myself walking over Canal Saint-Martin, going to my parents' door. I imagine myself showing my mother my dress, the one whose skirt is salvageable but which needs a new bodice because the old fabric is so threadbare it has holes.

"If I remake it a little it will at least be good enough for work," I say, taking it out of the dresser drawer where I have it shoved.

Nise comes over and looks at it with me. "There's a lot of good wear in the skirt," she says. "It would be pretty with a different fabric for the top."

Then I picture my mother's face. I take the trouble to see her in my mind's eye before I say the next thing. Before I tell the next lie.

"She'll know what to do with it," I say. "For certain."

So I am carrying my dress when I leave, when I walk up to the quai. And to be sure, I turn right on the quai, just the way I would if I were going to my parents' in Popincourt. But instead of walking all the way down to Pont de la Tournelle, I take Pont de l'Archevêché to cut over to la Cité.

While I'm on the bridge, a flock of starlings flies overhead, and I stop to watch. The flock turns this way and that, here and there, and if one bird strays from the edges of the group, it quickly comes back. I keep looking up in the sky even after they fly on.

Whatever it is in me that wants and wants—it is as big as the sky and keeps going.

H e *said just a little* farther north is the Plaine de Monceaux, and that it still feels like a village there—allées lined by trees, farmland, goat paths. But to me even his studio seems like it should be in a village. A window with sixteen tiny panes of glass tops the door, and the door itself is made of rough, wood planks. Ivy overgrows it, and the entire place looks a little tumbled down. I noticed the other day, but now I see it even more clearly. And yet I can also understand why he picked this place. If you wanted to try to get something done, away from other people, this is the sort of spot you would want. I am trying hard to understand what it all means to him because I know that it does mean something.

Maybe that is how my face looks when he answers the door, as though I am still trying to take things in. Or maybe I just look as unsure as I feel. All I know is that he seems surprised to see me.

Surprised, puzzled—something. But he should not be surprised, I think.

"Where is Denise?" he says when he shuts the door behind me. "Où est ta copine?"

"I didn't tell her I was coming."

"What did you tell her?"

"That I was going to see my mother. To do some sewing."

He looks at me after I say that, and he seems solemn. Serious. Maybe because I came on my own and it is no longer his fantasy of the brunette and the redhead. And yet I came on my own last night in the street, too, and he was glad. More than glad—I felt it from him.

I am not sure how to get back to the place we were on the street last night, when I ran to him and he was pleased to see me, but I know it has to do with acting as if everything is as it should be. So I walk further into his studio and then I know what to do.

I go to the divan and I lie down. Then I let myself look at him the same way I looked at everything I saw today when I walked up here—the streets, the birds, the sky. I let my eyes move over him as if I were looking at a plain or a river.

That is how we get back to the place we were last night on the street, when I ran beyond the dogleg of Maître-Albert, when he was a stranger from far away and not a stranger once I touched him.

He *half sits, half lies* on the divan and I am on top of him, my knees on either side. It feels odd at first to kiss him because no one else is here. I keep stopping because that is what I have always done, and then I realize I do not have to.

"What if she had come after you in the street last night and not me," I say. I do not want to say Nise's name, and I wonder if he will.

"She didn't come."

"If she had."

"I don't think you would have let her come alone," he says. "I don't think you would have ever let her come back down the street without you."

"No," I say. "I wouldn't have let her come."

"It counts more than you know."

"What does?" I say.

"To be wanted like that."

⚜

He kisses my breasts. First one and then the other. He holds each one in both hands, as if they were bottles he could tip back into his mouth.

After he tugs and sucks, he says, "I like how they feel in my mouth."

⚜

I'm the one who unbuttons his shirt.

"I want to see," I say. "I want to feel."

"Feel away," he tells me.

The forearms that I have held on to as we walked—they are covered with golden brown hair. His chest is like that, too. The hair is soft and silky, and again I smell the clove and orange scent I smelled the one night when we walked.

He must use cologne. This time the smell does not remind me of my mother.

⚜

He takes off my boots for me. He takes them off so I can take off my stockings, so I can be bare-legged on his lap.

"Those are my whore boots," I tell him. "A whore gave them to me."

"Who was she?"

"Someone my mother sewed for. La Belle Normande."

"Was she grand?"

"I thought so," I say.

"Lift up," he says then.

He keeps one arm around me and undoes his trousers with the other hand. Frees himself.

When I sit back down it is just my petticoat between us.

❦

There is a place at the base of his throat where the skin is very pale. It is a tiny indentation just above the breastbone and between the collarbones, a little scooped-out place that looks vulnerable.

Men look more vulnerable than women do when they are naked, I think. Or maybe I just think that because I know what my own body looks like.

When I look between his legs he does not look vulnerable. Does not look like anything but himself.

❦

I would have shared him with Nise. And if she wanted it, I would have touched her, too. It could have been the three of us, just like he always said.

But in the end he feeds the one whose mouth is open widest, who gets there first. That is what I tell myself.

He picks the hungriest one.

We stay together, *the two* of us on that narrow divan, until one or two in the morning, until he says, "I hate to, but I have to go."

He does not say the word *home*, but I know that is what he means.

"Stay here," he says. "I'd like to think of you staying here."

When I do not answer, he asks, "What is it?"

"I have to work tomorrow."

"Don't go."

"And then what," I say.

"There are other ways to earn money."

Before I would have said, *What would you know about it?* But I do not say that now. Instead I just tell him, "It's not that easy."

"I'll help you. Decide tomorrow. I'll come first thing."

I shake my head no, but I know I do not mean it because I do not stand up. I lie back on the divan, curl up under the blanket.

"Will you be all right here?"

"Yes. If you come back in the morning," I say.

"I'll be back before it's light."

He kisses me and then he is gone.

The whole time I am deciding to stay, it feels wrong, as if it is a foolish decision. I could have stood up, pulled on my dress and boots. Could have asked him for money to get home—he would have given it to me. But I did not do any of those things. Instead I let him decide for me.

The room seems cavernous with him gone. I feel some kind of fear flash through me for a moment—but there is no running after him this time. No running to find him because I'm half-dressed and I don't know which way he went.

So instead of doing anything, I just go still. I go on lying on the divan, letting my eyes move over everything in the room. I did not rush to pull on my dress and boots because I wanted to keep lying here. I thought I wanted him to stay, I thought it was just wanting the moment to go on, but now that he is gone, I see it is also something about being in this room and not going back to Maître-Albert. About breaking that life in two. I needed a place to be and he saw that.

Even without him in it, the room is him. I can be close to him without being with him. When that thought comes to me, I let myself close my eyes. If he were here I would never be able to think over things, but now I can. At first I think about the room on Maître-Albert and how I do not want there to be any hurt feelings, but I know there will be. I almost cannot stand to think of Nise there, alone. But she will come up with a way to explain it to herself. She will worry and then she will come up with the truth or a made-up story, and it will have to do.

I decide that and then I make myself let the thoughts go.

Instead I think about the ways he touched me, going back through each moment in my mind, playing it over and over. It is how I make sense of my feelings, of what just happened, but it works the way it always does: if I remember things right, it is almost as if I can feel the touch again. As if I have the feelings all over again.

I keep doing that until I remember the way he looked up at me from between my legs. His mouth was soft and scratchy at the same time because of the beard. I think of that, and of things he said. I think of it until I get sleepy, and then I let myself sleep.

⚜

When I wake up things are not even gray—they are still black with only lighter black coming through the window. So I wrap myself up in the blanket, light a candle and walk around, looking at the paintings he has hanging. What I see is:

A painting of a boy in a red hat with a bunch of cherries on a ledge. The cherries are wrapped in green paper, and some are falling off the edge. Even in the dim light I can see the boy's hat is a different color than the cherries. The hat is so brilliant it looks like a sun, or maybe I think that because the boy is fair and blonde, and his whole face is pale and shining.

The next painting is a man in a top hat with a glass beside him. He is wrapped in a cloak, and a bottle lies on its side at his feet. The man extends one leg, as if he were some kind of dancer, but that cannot be true. The man is not a dancer. That is not the feeling of the picture at all. But I do not know what the feeling of the painting is. The last painting was sunny, filled with gold and red, but this painting is dark. Just dark.

The next painting shows two old people, the man seated and the woman standing alongside. She keeps one hand in a basket of yarn, and he keeps one hand tucked inside his coat and the other clenched tight on the arm of the chair. The woman's eyes are downcast, not seeing. Yet you can tell from her face she is suffering. He looks out and seems strict. Disapproving.

The painting beside the one of the old people is much bigger. A man sits sideways, head wrapped in a white scarf, playing a guitar. He must be singing because his mouth is open. From its size, I know it must be important, but I do not know why.

The painting I look at next is probably half the size of the last, and yet it shows a crowd of people, some seated, some standing, all under trees in a park. The men are in top hats and the women in fancy dresses. This painting is dark, too, but here and there are patches of color: the pale gray of men's pants, the pink-gold ladies' gowns, a blue ribbon holding a bonnet. I look and I look, but hardly anything about the painting seems real. Only one woman has a complete face with eyes and eyebrows, a nose and a mouth—most of the rest have just hints of faces. And though the men's faces are more precise, only one man looks friendly in the entire sea of faces.

I look around the studio and think I have seen everything he has displayed, but then I see a couple of canvases he has sitting on a cupboard at the back, leaning and facing the wall. When I turn them around, I see both are paintings of women, but there is nothing similar about them. One shows a woman in an enormous white dress with gray stripes on it. The woman holds a black fan, and it seems she is sitting on the divan in the back of the studio. But there is something wrong with the picture, or with the woman herself. Her one hand is too big, her foot sticks out from her skirt, and her face seems flat and unmoving. She looks like a frightening doll. Her dark, flat eyes bother me, so I turn the painting back to face the wall.

So maybe it is just the relief when I look at the other painting, but I know as soon as I see it that it is my favorite of all. A woman in a white and gold blouse stands, resting her head against one hand, the other hand at her hip. Her skin is a darker gold than her blouse, and she has brownish-black hair and a white cigarette in her mouth. A white horse stands behind her, looking on, and he is patient-looking, the way the horse with the checkered sacks on Rue des Marmousets always is. And even though I like the white horse, of course I know it is the woman who makes the painting beautiful. I like the gold of her skin and blouse, and the deep red of her skirt, but what I like especially is her dark, messy hair and her face. I look at her face for a long time, and I think it is a little like looking at the faces of women at Baudon. It is a face I feel like I almost could know. And I think this is the painting he should have showed to Nise if he wanted her to understand how he felt about us, if he wanted the three of us to stay together.

It takes me a long time to look at just those seven paintings, and by the last I cannot look anymore. It is hard to take them in and to try to see whatever it is he wanted someone to see. I want to understand the paintings because he made them, but also because I do not understand how anyone can make daubs of color look like something other than what they are. How can you put paint on a canvas and make it look like a person's face or a fold of cloth or a piece of fruit? How can one person's face look like the face of a friend and another like an ugly doll?

I understood the funny little drawings of cats he showed us the first day because they were simple, lines and patches of shadow. But these paintings are not simple, and I do not know what he wants me to feel about the people in the pictures. The little boy with the cherries is pleasant and the old people seem sad, but I do not have any kind of feeling about the man with the bottle or the singer or any of the people in the park, under the trees. And yet I know there is something I should feel.

I am walking around the room, still wrapped in the blanket, trying to decide if I should lie down again, when I pass by the table by the front door and see the coins. He must have put the coins on the table as he left. Twenty francs. Not much to him but a ransom to me. No, not a ransom—but two weeks' wages.

And that is when I know he left the coins for me. I know he left them for me, or at least meant for me to see them. And I know I will not take them.

But seeing them makes me decide. In a couple of minutes I am dressed, and in another couple of minutes I ease the door open and look out at the half-light of the courtyard. I pull the door closed behind me so it latches, so I cannot change my mind. But I would not change my mind because whatever uneasiness I started to feel when I saw the money is now a panic about the time and the quartier and how long it will take me to walk home and get my work apron and my burnisher and make it to Baudon.

Because whatever he meant when he left the coins and whatever possible kindness it sprang from, it has some kind of opposite effect on me. There may be other ways to earn money but I know only one: *brunisseuse*. And twenty francs are a handsome gift but that is exactly what they are: a gift. Not a wage.

So I hurry into the morning and onto the streets that are perfect and empty and filled with a kind of coolness you never feel except first thing. I do not let myself think about how he touched me or the things he said, I do not let myself think about the way he uses color in the paintings to make everything from a person to an animal to a feeling, and I do not think about the money he left on the table, there for the taking. I just walk as quickly as I can in the cool down Malesherbes and Saint-Honoré and down to the river and then back home.

To my apron and my bloodstone.

get to Baudon late.

When I see Nise across the room she smiles at me, but it is a wan smile and I feel bad. When I get to go by her table, though, all she says is, "Late night?"

"That depends," I say.

And she smiles again but she does not say anything else. There is no time anyway.

At lunch she still does not say anything when we go out onto the street to buy bread and cheese. After a little while of the silence, I understand that she knows everything, so I say, "I thought it would be the three of us together. You and me and him."

"I never did."

"Didn't you want to be with him?"

"At first. But not like that. Not with you there."

I know it is only the truth. But something snaps shut in me

when she says it. Because I would have been with him and her. Because of the day she brushed my hair. Because I have always been a little in love with her faraway eyes.

"We don't need him," she says. "Don't you see that? Il nous perturbe."

I shake my head yes because I know she is right—he is disturbing us. But what exactly do I have that cannot be disturbed? The room on Maître-Albert? A life with no money in my pocket?

I want him to disturb me. That is the thing I want to tell Nise. But when I see her face I do not say anything. She would not be able to hear me anyway.

~∞~

After lunch Huberty tells me that I will not get paid for the morning.

"I was only half an hour late," I say.

"That's the penalty," he says. "You know that."

I do know—it was part of why I panicked this morning when I was up on Rue Guyot. But I thought if I just came in, if I came in close to the time, it would somehow work out.

"Why did I bother to come in then?" I say.

"You came in to keep your job."

When he sees my face, he shakes his head. "It's not my rule," he tells me.

Which I know. It is not up to him—it is just the way the shop runs. I try to take it in stride, try to just go back to smoothing out the lines of silver I made with the first pass of the burnisher. I focus on the thing underneath my fingers and when I find myself thinking of anything, I push it away the way I do the silver.

And I calm down. I do. At least it feels that way to me. Except nothing feels right. Women's voices cascade around me but I cannot really hear them, and something inside me keeps getting bigger. It makes me feel dizzy.

I stop working on a plate. I wrap my burnisher up in its cloth and shove the whole thing in my apron pocket. The front of my apron is wet but I do not take it off—I just keep my hand on the bundle in my pocket and I walk toward the side pulley-door.

That is how I leave.

I am out in the courtyard, ready to walk out onto Rue Pastourelle, when I hear her behind me.

"Where are you going?" Nise calls.

So I stop. Turn around.

"To his studio," I say.

"What are you going to do?"

"Something. Anything."

I have four francs and twenty sous in my pocket. My money, not his. I give the francs to her. "Take it for the room," I say.

It is not enough to help—it is just my half of the week's rent on the room. But it is what I have.

"What will you do?"

"He'll help me," I say. "He said he would."

"Why would you trust him? We were just a game to him. Don't you see that?"

"It's not like that," I say. "It's not like Moulin's."

We watch each other then. And I feel the thing I always feel when she looks at me. I feel the space her eyes create. I feel the air around my body.

"It would have been the way it always is," I tell. "Except he would have been there with us. He would have loved us both."

"You're a fool," she says, and she shakes her head at me. She shakes her head and shakes her head, and I know she is so angry with me she cannot speak. But when I go to hug her, she lets me. And that is how we say goodbye. Just two girls in aprons, hugging on the street.

Nothing anyone would want a picture of.

change out of my work dress and then pack my things, if you can call it that. I get my other dress, my two chemises, my underthings, my washcloth and towel, pillow, and the rags for my curse. My sketchpad and green boots. I take the scarf from the whore and the two pillowcases out of my trunk but I leave the trunk. Maybe Nise can sell it. I know I cannot carry it. I put everything in the pillowcases.

It takes me about as long to pack as it takes to climb the stairs to our room. That is how light I travel.

He is working when I get there. This time he is not surprised to see me, but I can see him taking all of it in: the bundles I am carrying, the breathless way I know I must look. I watch it all pass over his face. It makes me nervous but in a second I see he is not angry. Concerned. Annoyed, even. But not really angry.

"Did you and Nise have a falling-out?" is what he says.

I want to tell him, no, you were wrong, she and I are still friends. But I do not know if we are. I do know it is private, between Nise and me. So I just say, "I need to find a place to stay. Will you help me?"

"I came here to help you this morning."

When he says that I understand he is not upset with me because I showed up with my things, breathless—he is upset because I left.

"I saw your money," I say.

"I thought it would help you stay."

"But you didn't stay. So I told myself, *Go to work. Just go to work.*" And though I don't intend to, I end up telling him about Huberty and getting docked for the morning. About walking out of the shop. The whole day comes out.

"It's still there," he says when I am done. "Take it."

I go to the table and see the same thing I saw this morning. The coins still in the same place, just where I left them. Where he left them for me. But this time I do not hesitate. I pick up the money with both hands.

"I need this," I say.

And I think of the francs I gave to Nise and the room on Maître-Albert, and Huberty telling me I would not get paid for the morning, and I think I may just break down. But I do not. And I do not say anything else. I just stand there with his money in my hands.

He does not say anything and he does not come close. He stands still. I think he knows if he came close I would break.

I take the money from him just like I took his tongue on mine that one night. I take what he gives.

We're lying on the divan. He touches me, fingers me, and I touch him, too. I keep my hand around him.

"Can I tell you the truth about something?" he asks. He keeps his fingers in me as he says it, so I go on touching him, too.

"Yes."

"I already have one son I don't claim. I don't want to impregnate you."

I do not say anything but I do not have to. He can feel everything in me.

"Do you know things you can do?"

"Yes."

And I do know. Julie told me, and women talked about it all the time in the shop. Single girls and married women—it did not matter. Everyone knew some kind of method.

"I'll do something," I say.

"Can I go back here now?" he asks, and moves one of his fingers.

"Yes."

He touches the tight knot of me and slips his finger inside. And that is how it is for a while: I do not know where his fingers will go next, so I close my eyes. Let him play.

But he has only my wetness on him when he moves into me, and he goes in all at once. It hurts so much I yell for him to stop. I use the polite form. That is what comes out—*Arrêtez*.

So he does. He does not pull out of me—he just stops moving. I can feel everything beating in that place between us.

He kisses my shoulder blades, touches the sides of my breasts. I try to let everything go slack. Then I am more used to it. More used to the fullness there.

"Now," I say. "Now you can."

And he begins to move again.

After, *I am lying on* the divan and he stands beside me. I see one tiny piece of shit clinging to him, clinging to his cock, right at the head. It embarrasses me, though what do I expect. He looks down and sees it, too. Which shames me more.

But he calmly picks it off and then walks to the basin to wash.

"C'est pas grave," he tells me. "Men think their cocks are swords anyway. It's part of doing battle."

Modèle de profession—that is what he says I am. Or that is what we are going to call me as I stand there, putting on my garter.

"It saves me the trouble of going to Pigalle for a model," he says. "Or to Couture with his cast of characters."

"What do you want me to do?" I say.

"Nothing. Do what you usually do."

"Like this?"

"You don't have to look at me," he says.

So I look down and fiddle with the metal clip and the band. I keep my head lowered and when I get tired of pushing at my stocking, I let my fingers relax and just keep them there, the tips tucked under the band above my knee.

I know the tops of my breasts are showing, pushed up by my

stays, but when I go to tuck my nipple behind the edge of the fabric, he tells me not to.

"I need that bit," he says.

It all takes longer than the photographs at Moulin's, and that is the hardest part. How long it takes, and keeping still, especially my neck. Every once in a while I push my shoulders down in such a way that I do not change position—I just push with my muscles and then relax again. It must not change anything because he does not tell me to stop.

At first my mind keeps wandering but after a while, everything in me goes blank. I stand there with my head down and my hands at my knee, fingers tucked in the band of the garter. It is not comfortable, really, but it is somehow peaceful. When do you ever stand somewhere, not doing anything? Even when you wait for a train, you never stand totally still—you pace, you check, you look around.

Now I stand perfectly still except for pushing down my shoulder muscles and blinking. And it calms me.

I do not know how much time goes by. He does not talk and neither do I. I go off into my own self, and with my head down, I cannot even see him. It is like being away from him. As if I have left him somewhere. Yesterday there was so much give-and-take between us, and now that stops. Or it stops in one way, and in another way it goes on. Because of course I can feel him there, looking at me. Studying me.

"All right," he says then, and his voice sounds so peaceful I think he must have felt it, too. The relief at being silent, at not having to fill the air with words.

When he shows the pastel to me, I do not say anything. Maybe it is the not speaking, or maybe it is that I am still coming back from wherever I went in my head. But then I think no, it is seeing what he has drawn that does it. Even though the drawing does not show all of my face, it is clearly me. But it is also different from what I thought it would be. I have never seen my head bent, or the part in my hair, but even that is not what I mean. Somehow the drawing changes my picture of who I am.

"Is that really what I look like?"

"At this moment," he says. "To me."

I do not know how to talk about what I see, so I say, "Why did you make my stocking blue?"

"Because your hair is russet. Because the wall is yellow," he says. "Because white has blue in it anyway."

I am not sure I understand what he means, but it makes me think back to the day he added the reflection in the window on my drawing. That day he turned white paper into glass with gray pencil strokes. Still, all I really know is the blue stocking is maybe the prettiest thing in the drawing. Almost as pretty as the rounded tops of my breasts.

"Will you do anything else to it?"

"What do you mean?"

"Do you do anything to finish it?"

"Add a background to it."

"That's all."

"That's all. It's right from the start or it's shit."

"And my stocking is blue because my nipple's pink."

114

"The stocking is blue because your nipple is peach," he says, and then he puts the drawing down.

Peach, pink—I take off my stays so he can touch me. So I can feel his mouth on the color.

⌇

In the daylight, I notice something about him I did not see before.

Here and there on his cheeks, at the edge of his beard, I can see small scars—small pitted places. I cannot tell if the scarring gets worse because further down his beard is too thick.

He sees me looking so I say, "It's not bad. I don't know why you cover it up."

I tell him the tiny places remind me of a girl from Baudon. Everyone called her La Grêlée, the pockmarked one.

"She had a tiny patch on each cheek that looked as if it had been struck by hail. But it added something to her face."

"The name," he says. "Didn't she mind it?"

"She didn't seem to. She was still pretty."

"Even with the pocks?"

"You noticed the marks," I say. "But once you noticed, you realized you still thought she was pretty."

He looks at me when I say that, but I cannot explain it any better. I do not compare it to Nise's eyes, but to me it is the same. The flaw in what is pretty makes it more interesting.

Still, I think he would understand. After all, he fell a little in love with Nise, too.

❦

After I dress for the second time that day, I ask him about the paintings he has hanging on the walls of the studio.

"That was my assistant," he said, looking at the painting of the blond boy with the cherries. "And those are my parents," he says of the old couple.

"Is your mother sad?"

"I would say. In some ways her life hasn't been easy," he tells me.

I want to ask him why, but he goes on to the next paintings, the man with the bottle at his feet and the one playing the guitar, singing.

"Here is a failure," he says of the man in a cape with the bottle at his feet. "And this is a success," he says of the singer with the guitar.

"Why is one a failure and one a success?"

"Because this one is doused in the brown sauce I learned to paint with. Because I was too stupid to leave it behind."

He stands looking at the man with the cape and the bottle, studying the dark canvas, and then he says, "It's like seeing into a tomb, isn't it?"

I do not want to agree too much, but I also know I should not lie. Not about his paintings.

"It's very dark," I say, and nod at the painting.

"What else?"

"His foot seems odd," I say. "I don't know what to make of him."

"He's not a type you've seen in the street?"

"No."

"This one was at least a success," he says, and nods at the painting of the singer. "Everyone saw the influence of the Spaniards in it."

"Is he Spanish then?" I say. "The guitar player?"

"If Montmartre were in Spain," he tells me.

I want to ask him about the paintings of the two women on the table, the ones turned to face the wall, but I do not know if I should admit I turned them right way around. I think I should—I think I should just tell him the truth—but then I remember the strange doll's face of the woman in the white dress, and I do not know what I would say about her. So I walk over and stand in front of the painting of the crowd of people under the trees.

"Who are they?"

"The satin crowd at the Tuileries."

Of course it is easier to see more in the daylight, and now I know I was wrong about some of the things I thought I saw when I looked at the painting by candlelight. I did not even really notice the two little girls playing at the very bottom of the painting, though they are not so much real children as they are wisps of paint in the shape of children. But I was right about some things, too.

"Is that you?" I say, and point to one of the figures on the left.

"More or less."

"And is this man your friend?" I ask, pointing to the man that I thought looked like a friend the first night I saw him in the sea of faces.

"Fantin-Latour? Yes, he's a friend. But everyone in the painting is a friend or an acquaintance."

"So the painting's like a puzzle?"

"It didn't start that way," he says. "But it became that. An exercise."

"Well it's clear you like him. And it's clear you admire her," I say, and look directly at the only woman who has real features. "She's the only woman whose face you haven't covered."

"Madame Lejosne. Her husband is an officer."

He watches my face after he says that, and I can see from his eyes that I got it right: he does admire her.

"But you're partly wrong," he tells me then. "My mother is in that painting and I both love and respect her."

"She's your mother. You have to say that."

We go on looking, and he says the name of one fine man after another: Champfleury and Balleroy, Astruc and Scholl, and someone he calls *mon cher Baudelaire*. He does not identify a single one of the women except La Dame Lejosne and his mother, who is so heavily veiled you cannot see a single of her features.

"Is that who you're closest to?" I ask when he is done naming people. "Fantin-Latour?"

"He's a close friend but not the closest."

"If he's like he looks, he's the kindest one of all."

"He's young and handsome. You picked out the young romantic, that's all."

"But he is kind, isn't he?"

"I'm sure he would be kind to you," he says.

"Is Madame Lejosne kind?"

"Always. I visit her once a month in her home and I kiss her soft hand."

We stand together, watching each other. Regarding each other. The teasing has changed the air between us.

"Aren't you going to ask me about the two paintings on the table?" he asks me then. "I know you looked at those as well."

For a moment I am embarrassed. And then I decide not to be. He was the one who left me here that night, who trusted me. He must have known I would look.

"I liked the one," I tell him. "The gold woman with the white horse. The other woman frightens me."

"Why does she frighten you?"

"Her face looks like a doll's face. An ugly doll's face."

He looks at me for a long time before he speaks, and then he says, "She's the mistress of a friend. She was once very beautiful, I think. Now I think she's miserable."

"Because of him?"

"He can be cruel. But she's miserable because she's sick. And because they never have enough money."

"Does your friend like the painting?"

He does not answer at first and then he shakes his head no. Tells me, "I would have given it to him if he had."

"Why did you paint it if you don't care for her?"

"Because he asked. And then she came here and sat, and I couldn't do anything but paint what I saw."

"With him looking on?"

"With him looking on," he says.

He walks over to the table then, and I think for a moment he will turn around the painting of the woman in the white dress, but he does not. Instead he turns the painting of the woman in the gold blouse. In the light I can see what I did not see by candle: that the gold blouse is both gold and flame orange, that the white at the front of the blouse is not the white of the horse but is the white of the cigarette, that the blue of the sky is gray in places and purple in others.

"Why would you turn this to face the wall?"

"Because I can't bear to hear what people say about it. About the brushstrokes and the composition. About the girl herself. You can't paint people like that, people at the edges, or if you do you can't show the beauty in them. They have to be caricatures, like Daumier's."

I do not understand what he is getting at—the ideas go beyond me. But I say, "Is she someone special then?"

"She was just a girl I saw at Porte de Clignancourt. Probably a gypsy."

When he says it—that is when I know he loves the painting. And that is when I know that if he loves something, he hides it.

Even though I am dressed and thought I was leaving, I let him pull me back to the divan at the back of the studio, the same divan where he and Nise and I sat kissing, the same divan where the white doll of a mistress sat for him. And I undress for the third time that day.

⁓

The divan is not a bed, but still.

I know I liked it when my soldier held me on the cushion of his thighs and made the wall behind us a room. But it is a different kind of pleasure to be able to stretch out beside someone. To take time with his body, and come to know it.

And if I could draw him, this is what I would draw:

When he sits on the divan, there is one place on the side of his hip that curves in. I know it is just from him sitting, just the way the muscles of his hip come together with the muscles of his leg, but that curve inward, that small indentation with its shadow, bewitches me, and I like to press my mouth there.

Veins in his forearms track over the muscle like vines. The vein-vines are soft when I trace them, first with my finger and then with my tongue. He has the same kind of veins that show over his cock.

I trace those, too.

That is what I would show in a drawing. Just shadows and lines.

he sponges are the size of walnuts or small apples. Golden brown. Dry, I cannot believe they can be used for that purpose, but when I wet one, it makes sense. The sponge comes alive in the water. The surface silky, like hair underwater. When it is wet I can imagine it going inside me, I can imagine it fitting exactly where it needs to fit. Nestling up there. Each one has a long silk ribbon threaded through it. That is how you get them out.

When I try one, it feels like tucking some kind of damp flower up there. I have to use my middle finger to push it all the way up, until I hit the "nose." That is what Adèle said the tip of it would feel like when I touched it. That is the part to cover.

When the sponge is in I don't feel anything—just the tickle of the ribbon on my thigh.

It is the ribbon I show him.

"Do you have to use any powders with it?" he asks.

"Druggists sell them. Adèle said she used vinegar and water."

"So that's what you did?"

"Does the smell bother you?"

"It doesn't bother me," he says.

The whole time we are talking, I have my legs spread open and he pets me there. Smoothing the hair and fingering the ribbon. That is when I understand it is all part of the game to him. Part of the pleasure. I did not have to squat behind the screen to put the sponge in—I know that now.

"What do you do at the end?"

"Wash it out and soak it in vinegar for a while. Vinegar again."

But he is already starting to move into me when I tell him that. Still dressed in his shirt and blue cravat. Lavallière bleue à pois blancs. He got his pants down and that was all, like some coureur on the street.

"So you have a bit of the sea inside you," he says to me when we are done, when we lie together, still joined.

"A bit of the sea and a bit of you," I say.

❧

"*What is he* to you?"

That is what Adèle asked when I talked to her about not getting pregnant. It took me a second to answer, *a lover.*

Not *my lover*—a lover. That is all.

When I tried to explain, she said, "So there's money involved. Il y a toujours de l'argent."

"Paris is full of whores," I say. "I know. But it's not just that."

"What is it then?"

"True love," I told her, and we both laughed like we used to at Baudon.

But it is not so simple. He and I are not so simple.

If he wanted a whore he could have paid one, and if he wanted two whores together, he could have paid them both instead of spending all that time on Nise and me. He chose not to. All that is true, but it is still not what I mean.

What I mean is that it is not always so clear what someone wants, or what money can buy, or who exactly pays.

When I was twelve or thirteen, when I sat at home and listened to my mother talk with the women who came to her with sewing, I remember them talking about a whore named Mezeray who had been killed in her bed. The story was in all the papers. It was not one of her customers who killed her but a young gardener named Guichet, from Vaugirard. Someone she had taken a fancy to and brought home to her bed. He made love with her, and then the two of them went to sleep. And sometime during the night he woke up and killed her.

He cut her throat with his pruning hook. Not even a knife—a pruning hook. And after he killed her, he washed his shirt in her basin and took some of her things. He sold them and went back home to Vaugirard. When they found him he was drinking with the money from her things and cleaning his pruning hook.

He told the judge he woke up once in the night wanting to kill her, but he did not do it then because she woke up, too. She woke up and turned to him in the bed and kissed him. So he had to wait.

The person who hurt Mezeray was not someone who paid for her, who thought she was a thing to buy. It was Guichet, whom she took to her bed not for money but for someone to hold and kiss. But he went to her bed not for sex or the illusion of love, but for the money he could get for her things. And in the end it was she who paid, the so-called whore, and not in cash but with her life.

Une bête, my mother said when she heard the story. *Un vrai sauvage.*

So maybe it is true, maybe Adèle is right that it is always about money—le fric, le blé, le pognon, l'argent. Whatever you call it. I just mean that things are not as clear as they first seem.

He tells me he wants me to wait to put in the sponge.

"If you put it in before, all I can taste is vinegar," he says.

So we keep the sponge in a little pan of vinegar and water beside the divan. A sea creature in its own shell.

The room is on *Rue* La Bruyère. It is another climb to the sixth floor, but this place is lighter than the one on Maître-Albert. There is a dormer window you can actually see out, across the courtyard to another building whose whole backside is painted white with HERBORISTE in black letters.

I do not know why but I like to see the sign. It is the first thing I check for in the morning and one of the last things I see before I sleep. It is always there.

I put the scarf from the whore on the table underneath the window. Put my sketchbook there, along with the candles. *Veilleuse Astrale, brûlant 10 heures.*

He pays for the room for a month, and the first time he comes to see me there, I tell him he can stay with me whenever he wants.

"I will sometimes."

"Where do you live?"

"A hotel room," he says. "Sometimes with the mother of my son."

"You aren't married to her?"

"No. I'm not married to her."

"Do you love her?" I say.

"I care about her and the boy. More than I care about anyone."

He tells me the boy is ten, that he is a fine boy. Merry and serious at the same time.

"I think it must be the situation," he says. "The ridiculous lies his mother and I tell. Or maybe it's my father coming out in him."

"Was your father merry?"

"Hardly. Severe. Plutôt sévère. He's still alive."

"What's wrong with him?"

"A multitude of things," he says, and I think of the painting he has hanging on the wall of his studio of his mother and father. The misery in the two faces.

"Were you in love with her once?" I ask then. "With the boy's mother?"

"I met her when I was seventeen. She had a white throat and thighs like columns."

"What happened?"

"Nothing. She's a wonderful mother. You could sleep on her bosom."

"All women have bosoms," I say.

"You don't."

"What do I have then?"

"Tits," he tells me. "Tits that fit in my hands."

꙳

After, we lie on my bed and I am closest to the wall. I look out over his chest to the window, and I can still see HERBORISTE. I think it is seeing that word that makes me ask. After that night at Flicoteaux's, I kept saying the word *Sallandrouze* in my mind, over and over, so I would not mispronounce it, so I could keep it in my memory.

"What happened at the Sallandrouze?" I say.

He has been moving his hand over my belly, stroking the hair down there, but now his fingers stop moving.

"Why do you ask me that now?"

"Because I've been remembering the word."

"Why?"

"Because you wouldn't tell the real story that night," I say. "Because Nise said she didn't want to hear it."

"I wouldn't have told you anyway."

"But it meant something to you."

He shifts on the bed, then, turning so he can lie flat on his back. So he can look up at the ceiling. At first I think he is not going to say, that he will refuse to tell me just as he did that night. But then he starts to talk.

"They did things in plain sight. They shot at anyone. Women and children. Not just people on the barricades."

"That's what you saw at the Sallandrouze?"

"We saw executions there. Tonin and I. One man was killed because soldiers said his hands smelled of gunpowder."

129

He stops talking then, but I do not say anything. I understand it is better not to say anything.

"The next day I went with my class to the cemetery at Montmartre," he says after the pause. "We went to draw, if you can believe it. And I saw someone I knew. The man I used to buy soap from. He was a merchant. That's who I drew."

"He was dead?"

"They'd covered the bodies with straw. Left the heads out in the open so you could see. And I saw him."

He waits a moment and then he says, "He was probably out running an errand, or just going about his business. It was butchery. All of it. Soldiers were drunk with blood. I don't talk about it. Not even to Tonin."

I want to say something more but I do not know what. There is nothing to say. I put my hand on his chest and lie beside him in the narrow bed.

"You're the last person I would have thought I'd tell," he says after a while.

"Why did you?"

"Because you asked. Because you're young and you should know."

Even though I have not felt young the way he means for a long time, I know I am. So I nod. At first I think I cannot think of anything to say, but then I do think of something.

"What was the man's name?" I ask. "The one who sold you soap?"

"Monpelas. He was a perfumer on Rue Saint-Martin. I used to buy sandalwood soap from him. Now I can't stand the smell."

Both of us are quiet after that. That is when I wonder if I should have carried the word *Sallandrouze* in my mind, if I should have asked him to tell me the story. But I cannot take the question back, and he cannot take the story back.

And because I do not know what else to do, I crawl on top of him. I kiss him hard, bump my teeth against his. When he begins to move inside me, there is nothing soft about it. It is hard and almost hurts.

In that way I take the story from him. I take it inside me, too.

Tonight we go walking down Boulevard Saint-Martin and over to Boule du Temple to see the street performers. I wanted to come walking here one night when it was still him and Nise and me. We would have been part of the spectacle, the three of us, with him in his ugly-fine coat and the two of us on his arms. But we never did. As it is, he and I fit in like any of the other lovers, soldiers and maids, workers together, but it is come now or not at all—almost the whole of the Boulevard du Crime is to be torn down, he says.

"Just like la Petite-Pologne," he says. "We could have gotten you a bed there for two sous a night."

"A bed and bedmates," I say, and pretend to pick a louse or two from his jacket, but he grabs my hand.

We stop in front of some jugglers and a sword swallower, and he stands behind me, the crowd an excuse to press close.

I feel him there behind me, and that sensation mixes in with watching the sword swallower's throat work behind a white kerchief.

After the sword swallower finishes with his blade, we move further down the street and find a strongman. The strongman stands there, shirtless, and that itself is a surprise, but even more surprising is how ordinary he looks. He has a thick neck and is barrel-chested, but he looks no different from many of the men in the crowd. And yet he is different somehow, too. He seems to roll on his feet as he walks, and when he talks it is as if he knows every single one of us in the crowd.

We watch as he slips a wooden yoke over his shoulders. On each end of the yoke, a circle of wood hangs from three ropes, making two small seats. He tells the crowd he needs two helpers to help him show his strength.

"Two men," he says. "Or girls if you like," and when he says that the crowd laughs and calls.

"Non, non, messieurs-dames," he says, and extends his arm to a worker in a blue smock. "I have my first. This voyageur."

The man in the smock steps forward and stands beside the strongman. And once the worker in the smock is part of what is to take place, he looks over the crowd too, a kind of performer himself.

"I'll know him when I see him," the strongman says, eyes moving over the bodies in the crowd, judging their willingness and their weights. When the man looks our way and makes his face a question, I'm sure he will shake his head no and tell the strongman to move on without a word.

But he does not. Instead he nods and then he moves from the warm place at my back. Steps forward to stand on the other side of the yoke, opposite the worker in his smock.

And that is the trick: a man on each seat of the yoke, suspended from the strongman's shoulders.

It begins with the seats up on two low blocks and the strongman in between. Each man takes his spot on the small wooden circles, but the ropes are slack. The strongman waits until the volunteers settle in, until each feels secure on the wood circlet, then he says, "Eh bien, hold on."

And he squats down, right between the two seats, and settles the wooden yoke on his shoulders. He tests the yoke one time against his neck and then begins to stand. It is a strain—clearly it is a strain— but there is no real hesitation. Just a slow movement upward as the strongman steadies the weight of the men on his shoulders and holds the top of the ropes where they knot in the yoke.

When he is upright, standing firmly, he looks out at the crowd, and we all holler and clap. The two men on the seats look outward, too, but they sit still, feet off the ground, not willing to move or break the balance. The crowd is shouting and clapping, and the strongman's face triumphs, but the two on the roped seats keep their serious expressions.

And then the strongman sets them down.

When we clap that time, it is for the strongman but it is also for them, the willing voyageurs, the perfect accomplices who did not even risk changing the weight of their faces with a smile. And as he makes his way back to me, I can feel the crowd turning to look at me, to look at my face as he walks toward me. Whatever we are to each other, something shows on my face and on his face, and the crowd sees it, and knows.

And I feel the crowd watching as he walks toward me, so I put my arms out to welcome him back from the daring feat and his time on the wooden circle but mostly so I can be close to him again. And when I kiss him on the mouth people shout and clap, and he and I are part of the spectacle on the street.

I think that feeling stays with us the rest of the night because whenever we stand watching something, he stands behind me, his arms linked up close under my breasts, like all the other sweet-hearts, like all the soldiers and their girls, and the workers and their women. He is my petit ami and I am his chérie, and I feel him against me all night.

By the time we get home, to my room on La Bruyère, we have been touching all night, and there is no modesty. He strips and lies down on my bed. When I ask him to help me with the damp flower of the sponge, he takes it from my hand and works it up expertly inside me. There is the vinegar sharp smell between us but it is all part of the whole, now. And then I am ready and he moves into me and it is slick, slick, slick.

~∽~

That night he stays with me.

At some point I feel him move away from me. I watch as he gets up, and I think he is about to dress, about to pull on his clothes and make his apology. Instead he goes and stands at the window.

"It's raining," he tells me.

"I hear it."

When he comes back to the narrow bed, he says, "It's good to be someplace when it's raining."

He lies back down beside me and we sleep until the morning, until I take him to Raynal's Café for breakfast. Fifty centimes for the two of us.

The next time I come to sit for him, I wear the dress I used to wear to Baudon, and I fix my hair the way I did for work, which is to say I leave it dirty and pull it back from my face. When I get there I know I have done it right because he nods at me.

"I want to get that working girl," he says.

I stand in the spot he shows me and turn my head just a little to the left, but he tells me not to look in that direction.

"Look back at me," he says. When I do, he nods and does not talk again.

So it is a glance he is painting. A sidelong glance. At least that is the way it feels.

And that is the thing that ends up aching about the pose—not my neck or shoulders but my eyes. The muscles in my eyes get sore and my eyes themselves start to dry. I can feel the air on the tissues. So I blink but each time I do, I look back to the exact same spot on the wall, just beyond his shoulder.

And just like the other time, in a little while my mind finds somewhere to go. I start off thinking about the strongman and the crowd, the serious way he and the worker in his blue smock looked when they took their perches on the circlets of wood hanging from the strongman's yoke. And then I fall into thinking about Nise, and how she always liked seeing the birds that did tricks on the boulevard, and then I am thinking about Toucy and her kid, and the flowers her mother had growing up strings next to her kitchen window. The flowers I drew in my carnet de poche. Now that I have seen his paintings and heard him talk about color, how one color needs another, color is all I can see. It is why the purplish blue of delphiniums looks good with their green leaves.

Once I start thinking of that, I think of every flower I can: lilacs, hyacinths, oeillets, honeysuckle, alyssum, coquelicots, nasturtiums, bluets, violets, pansies, lily of the valley, morning glories, roses and peonies—peonies which sometimes smell more like roses than roses do. But that still is not enough, so I go through the alphabet and try to think of flowers for different letters, and that way I pick up acacia, anemone, aster, camellia, chamomile, chicory, cinquefoil, clematis, clover, columbine, daffodil, daisy, dogsbane, flax, foxglove, gentian, gillyflower, goldenrod, heliotrope, jasmine, jonquil, lavender, lily, linden, lobelia, love-in-a-mist, love-lies-bleeding, lupine, madder, marigold, mignonette, nightshade, orchid, primrose, soapwort, sweetpea, tansy, valerian, veronica, viola, and wisteria. It takes a long time to come up with the list, and to come up with a picture of each of the flowers in my mind, and where I was the last time I saw it, and in that way hours go by. And when I get all the way through the alphabet, I think about the Marché aux Fleurs on the Île, and how tomorrow is Sunday and the bird sellers and rabbit sellers will be there with their wooden cages—

"Ça y est," he says, breaking me out of my thoughts. And when I hear his voice I close my eyes and keep them closed a long time, and what I see is not his studio or him but the marché with its small cages and flowers, all of it there on the quai, there in my mind's eye.

When I look at the painting—when he brings me around to see what he has done of it so far—I know everything I was thinking about is there in my eyes. The strongman is there, and Nise, and flowers, and the flower market, but also the quietness of the studio and the air between us.

It is all in the paint. It is all in the expression on my face.

"I like my eyes the best," I say, and he nods.

The blue bow in my hair, the fancy blouse, the black ribbon around my neck—all that gets added in after I sit for a while, resting, after we both eat bread and cheese back by the cupboard at the rear of the studio and drink one glass of wine. A blue bow because my hair is reddish orange. A black ribbon around the neck to contrast with the cream of my skin.

Still, when I am putting those things on, even though I partway know the answer, I say, "Why didn't you just have me wear this from the start?"

"Because you would have been different."

I understand, I do—the frippery would have made me feel different, or stand differently, and if he had told me he wanted me to wear a bow, I might have washed my hair and fussed with it.

But now that I understand, it isn't necessary. Now I understand that what matters is honesty. What matters is where I go in my head.

So in a little while I say, "Just ask for what you want. I'll give it to you."

He looks at me for a long while after I say that, and I think he will say something. But he does not. He just goes back to placing paint.

⌇

When the painting is done, we look at it together the way we did with the pastel drawing. This time I can see the focus is not my breasts or a blue stocking but my face.

Just my face.

I look plain. Not ugly, but not pretty, either. My lips are pale, my eyelashes light, and I can even make out the faint dimple in my chin. I look at all those things, I do, but I keep going back to my eyes. He has made them gray-green, and as I go on looking at them, I think I have never seen that color. And I think that must be why he made the rest of the painting so simple. Why he would not let me do my hair, why he kept my face naked. Yes, I am wearing a bow in my hair and a ribbon on my neck, but for some reason I hardly notice those things.

There is nowhere to look in the painting except my eyes.

And this time I know it is really how I look, not because I have seen my face that way but because I know what it feels like to look that way.

When my mother would not speak to me. When my grandmother died. When my heart was broken.

So this time it is a different question I ask. This time I ask, "Is that how you see me?"

He says, "When you let me."

t is after that painting that I start wearing the black ribbon. Not just when I sit for him—all the time.

I do not know if it belonged to someone else or not—it was in his studio the day he painted my portrait. It does not matter. It belongs to me now.

Sometimes I tie it in front, the way it was in the painting, and other times I turn it into a choker with the ends trailing down my back. Sometimes I wear it in my hair. I wear it for days, until it smells of my skin and hair, and then I wash it out in my basin. Borrow an iron to iron it.

Of course he notices it. And of course he knows I took it.

"It suits you," he tells me. That is all he ever says about it.

This time the photos he shows me are not from Moulin.
There is no art to it, no pretend poses of awkward girls with
their skirts pulled up or side views of breasts. There is one focus
only: the cocks of the men rising up into the women.

I know he shows the photos to me to shock, and they do. Even
when I tell myself not to let it show on my face, I know it does.
And after the first couple, I only half look.

It is not just the naked bodies that disturb me. The faces disturb me. A flat-faced woman who looks stupid or half-witted, and
all the men with dark mustaches. It all repulses me. And I know
that is part of it too: he wants to see my reaction.

After five or six photos I want to tell him to put them away,
that whatever it is he wanted, he got. But then the photos change
and for some reason I do not look away.

It is not the woman, who is prettier than the others, with flowers in her hair and some kind of necklace. It is the man. He is the reason I do not look away.

In the first photo he is in profile, and I can see his collarbone, the way the muscles in his neck lead down to it like cords. His hair is longish and brushed back, and he is handsome. Clean-shaven. Young. And his face. His eyes are downcast or facing the woman in all the photos, but you can still sense what his eyes are like. There is a calmness there.

In one photo he leans back in a chair, head propped up on one fist. He gazes down at the woman, who sits below him, sucking him. The look on his face is one of—not love, I would not claim that—but seriousness. Patience. Some kind of devotion.

"These aren't like the rest," I say. "The rest are fake."

"You don't think these are fake?"

"These two are lovers. Real lovers. Not just for the pictures."

"Why?"

"Look at his face," I say.

He watches me for a little while and then he says, "They could be lovers. Or you might just like him. Like the look of him."

"I like his face."

"Not his body? He's got quite a cock."

But I think the photos cannot show what is not there.

I think the sweetness and patience in the man's expression come from whatever he feels for the woman and the body of the woman. It is not something a photographer paid for. But what he says is also true: I like the body of the man in the photograph. I like his bare chest and his thighs. His sex. But without the expression on his face I would feel nothing.

So I say, "Yes. I like him. None of the others compare."

I face him when I say it and let his eyes read mine. And I can tell that I passed some kind of test. Because I told the truth. Because I was bold enough to tell the truth.

He does not know that I will think of the photos for a long time, or that I will picture the man's face and neck and cock in my mind, over and over. I'll think of it the same way I did when he said, *The redhead can take it.*

At first I could not believe the lewdness of his words, but in the days that followed, it was all I could think of. The way he looked at me and the way his voice sounded. It took me a while to understand my feelings, but then I did. As shocked as I was, his words also excited me. It is part of what drew me to him—that he would dare to say something like that. That he would say it to me and then watch my face.

What he said was crude. Raw. Yet once I heard it, I craved it.

N|ow *when I walk down* the street I notice different things.
Because of him.

How can it be that someone changes your eyes? The way you see?

Today it is a sign on a narrow strip of building that extends just beyond its neighbor, the brick only wide enough for single words:

CHEVALETS

TOILES

PALETTES

ET

COULEURS

FINES

am changing out of a gold cloak at the end of one day when he says, "You can take a break tomorrow. I don't need you. I have some other things I have to take care of."

He says it as ordinarily as he would say any words, so I make my voice ordinary, too, and say, "A day off. That will be nice."

I do not let anything show on my face.

When he kisses me goodbye and walks me to the door of the studio the way he always does, I can see he is already gone. Already absent.

I do not know how I feel anyway. Something about hearing him say *I don't need you* upsets me, but I tell myself it is about work only. That when I had the day off from Baudon I was happy.

So the next morning after I go to Raynal's for breakfast, I set out walking. I tell myself I have the day to myself to do as I please. At first it is fine because I think about everything that has happened with him, and how I feel closer to him than I ever thought I would, that it gets easier to talk each time we see each other. I like the days spent in the studio, the quietness but also the intensity.

A place could not be more different from Baudon than his studio, and my days could not be more different than they were.

But all I have to do is flash upon Baudon, and I begin to think about Nise, too. I think about the lie I told her, I think about money, and I think about how all the money I now have comes directly from him. He makes a point never to count coins into my hand—the francs are always waiting on the table, stacked neatly. I do not know if he does that for me, so I can take the money freely from the table and not directly from his hand, or if he does it for himself so he does not have to put the coins into my hand.

Probably he does it for both reasons.

It all begins to run together, the lie and Nise and the money he leaves counted out for me, and even though I am walking down streets, it seems like I am walking inside my own thoughts. I know it will not help if I sit down or turn around and go back to La Bruyère, though, so I keep on. In a little while I decide to go by Baudon to see if I can catch Nise, and once I decide that, some of the swirling inside me stops.

By the time I get to Rue Pastourelle it is almost lunchtime, and this time it is me hanging about in the street, waiting, the way he used to. I stand on the corner opposite the side of the street that Baudon is on, and I stand halfway down the block past where the soup seller has set up. I feel odd about being there, but I think about what I want to tell Nise and what I want to ask.

Mostly, I just want to catch sight of her. See for myself that she is all right.

When a group of women comes walking down the street from the side entrance, it takes me only a second to spot her. She is with a couple of the apprentices and Toinette, who worked at the table beside her. The four of them walk together to buy lunch, and it is Toinette she talks to. A few feet away from the soup seller, she and Toinette play-fight, jockeying to see who gets in line first, elbowing each other, talking and laughing.

I see all of that and I hear her laughing with Toinette before I turn away, before I move quickly on down the street, before anyone sees me from across the way. And something in me stings for the second time since he told me *I don't need you,* though I do not know why I should feel that way. What did I expect? That she would be walking by herself? Nise and I were always friends with Toinette. Always.

When I am safely away, I wonder if I really meant to talk to Nise anyway.

I thought I had something planned, but now I do not know what I would have said. Would I have shown her my new dress, bought because I wanted something that didn't have the armpits rotting out from so much washing? Told her about the sketches he did yesterday of me holding a guitar, as if I were some kind of singer?

It all seems so foolish I can barely stand it. I seem so foolish I can barely stand it. But I do not let myself think anything more until I get farther away.

I do not know how long that swirling feeling goes on. I do not even know it has stopped until I am walking down one street and realize that the conversation I have been having in my mind all morning has stopped repeating. When I hear the silence in my head, I slow down.

I wanted to go to Baudon to see her and speak with her. I thought I would know what to say. But something about seeing her with Toinette and the other girls—something about seeing them all together, and me being on the other side of the street, standing alone in the middle of the day with nothing to do—it took the courage from me. She would have teased me about my new dress, or what I was doing alone if I was now with him, or she might have been angry with me, and that might have been good. Maybe if she teased me or been angry it would have righted things, would have paid me back a little for my lie. And if I had picked any other day maybe that would have been fine, I would have gone up to her and let her tease me.

But just now I could not. Not with Toinette there. Not on a day when I feel so odd and out of place.

And I tell myself, *At least you saw her, and now that you know she is all right you can let go, you can.* But before I let go I know there is one more thing I need to think of. About her and about me.

Right after I moved into the room on Maître-Albert with Nise, something happened that I could not explain. I did not understand at the time, but Nise knew. And then I knew, too.

At first I thought it was just a regular period, but my head and whole body ached, and I bled so much it ran down my legs and into my boots. When I told Nise what was happening, she told me to lie down and press on my belly. So I did. She got me some rags and tucked them under me, and I lay on the bed and pressed with my fists, right above my mound.

In a little while the worst of the bleeding stopped, but not before I passed a blood clot the size of my fist. It came out onto the rag I had wedged under my hips on the bed. I saw it and it was the size of my palm.

Nise wrapped up the clot and carried it out in our slop bucket. I do not know if she took it to the trash or to the toilet in the hall, and she did not say.

"Je pense que tu fais une fausse couche," she told me when she came back.

I nodded when she said it, but it still did not make sense. I had been sleeping with someone, but I had not even missed a period. Had not seen anything except the clot.

When I said that to her, she said, "Maybe that's all it is when it's early. Just blood."

Then it did make sense. I did not have other words for what poured out of me except the ones she gave me, and I did not have another person to help me. And I do not just mean a person to help me understand. She got me a basin of clean water so I could wash, and she helped me scrub the blood from my skirt and wipe the blood out of my boots.

I said we were like sisters, but we were closer than that because sisters often fight, and she and I never did. We just loved each other and helped each other. We did not fight until the end, about him.

I walk and walk. More slowly now that my mind is not swirling, but I know enough not to stop altogether. As long as I keep walking, the streets keep me company. And I go on walking until I get to the Rue de L'Essai, there by the Marché aux Chevaux.

I remember the place from coming here with my father, and I look for the strange trees that grow just past the wall, there in the aisle of the marché. They look different now because they have leaves on them, but I still recognize them: branches on one side only, growing away from the building, with knobs of twigs reaching upward. When I was little and saw the trees in winter, I thought the branches looked like knuckles with fingers.

I walk up and down l'Essai and Poliveau, Duméril and Cendrier. Find the building that has the crane and the rooster on it. When I find that I feel better, and part of me wishes I had my carnet de poche along. I would not be able to draw the building or the plaque with the crane or the trees the way I really see them, but a drawing would be a record of the day. No matter what the drawing looked like, it would mean something.

But I have nothing with me, so all I can do is stand and look. I do that for a long time.

And when I finally walk away to begin to make my way home, something inside me does not ache so much. So it must be enough just to see things sometimes. Just to look and see.

When I go back to the studio the next day, he is done with sketches and wants to begin working on the painting where I have a guitar over my shoulder and eat from a paper cone of cherries. Except there is a problem. For the sketches we made do with a crumpled piece of paper, but now he really wants fruit, and that is where things become complicated. Cherry season is over.

"We'll have to improvise," he says.

So he sends me out to buy grapes instead. And when I come back, that is what he has me stand and hold and pretend to eat. A bunch of grapes.

"What did you do yesterday?" he asks after he has been working for a little while.

"I walked."

"Where to?"

I do not tell him I went to Baudon or that I saw Nise. "The Marché aux Chevaux," I say.

"All the way there?"

"Once I started I kept going."

"No wonder you look tired today," he says. "I think you wore yourself out."

"Well, once I got there I had to come home."

He laughs when I say that. It is a relief to hear him. To be standing in front of him, there in the quiet room.

A relief to have him see me.

When he is done for the day he steps away from the canvas, and that is when I can come and look.

Even though he made the sketches the other day, he did the painting today. That is how he works: sketch after sketch to prepare, and then the painting all at once, or as much as he can. So it stays fresh, he says. And though he painted me today, what I mostly see in my face is yesterday. The hand holding the cherry-grapes hides my mouth, but my face, at least what you can see of it, looks a little tired. Yet it suits the painting.

I do not want to talk about the day before to him, so I say, "The cherries in this painting are different."

"Too much like grapes?"

"No, I mean they're different from the cherries you painted for the boy in the red hat. The ones falling off the ledge."

When he looks at me, I realize he does not know I think about his paintings all the time. Mostly the gypsy girl, but all of them, including the blond boy with the cherries.

So he gets that painting and carries it back to the easel to compare.

The cherries in front of the boy and falling off the ledge are bright red. Tomato red. The ones I am holding are more subdued. Blackish red, like a real cherry would be—except I have been holding grapes.

"You're right," he says. "I knew they were different but I didn't know how different."

To me it almost looks as though he painted two different moods. The painting of the boy is light and cheerful, and the painting of me is serious. Subdued. But all I say is, "His cherries match his hat."

We stand there a while longer, looking at the paintings, and it feels nice. Standing together and looking at color.

"My cherries are the color of your pin," I say.

"What pin?"

I point. "Your cravat pin."

He looks at the painting of me and down at his chest and back to the painting. Says, "You have a good eye."

The words are kind—a compliment. But that is not all they are. Because right now, he looks the way I think Nise and I must have looked the first day he showed up at Baudon. Caught out. I caught him at something, and it takes me just a moment to understand what it is.

For the first time I think he realizes I notice small things. For the first time I think he understands that I have been studying him, too.

༜

"*I want to* tell you an ugly thing about that boy," he tells me after I dress, after I change out of the cloak and hat I was wearing for the painting and am back in my street clothes.

"The cherry boy?" I say. "He wasn't just a model?"

"He was my helper at the last studio. A boy from the neighborhood who ran errands for me. I took a liking to him and I thought I might influence him. He wasn't bad, really, but he often told lies. Anyway, one day when I came back to the studio I found him. He'd hanged himself. Just a thin cord—he was small. I'm the one who cut him down."

When he finishes, I wait a while before I say anything. Then I ask, "Why did he do it?"

"I don't know. He always seemed to be daring. Always pulling pranks."

"Maybe all his pranks were him trying to get noticed," I say.

He looks at me then, but he does not say anything, and it seems as though he wants me to go on. To tell him something more.

So I say, "Maybe he got tired of trying to be noticed. Maybe he decided he couldn't try anymore."

"Why couldn't he try anymore?"

"Maybe he wished for something and one day realized it couldn't be," I say.

"I don't know what he would have wished for that would be so dire."

"Maybe he wished he could be your boy," I say.

"Maybe," he says, and looks away. "Anyway, that's why I changed studios. That's why I moved up here."

He does not look back at me but stares out the window instead. And I know that, without meaning to, I somehow hurt him with my words.

"Don't listen to me," I say. "Who knows what people wish for."

He finally looks back at me when I say that, and sees that I am watching him.

"No," he says. "I think you know a great deal."

He holds his hand out to me then and I take it. And we stand there for a long time. Just holding hands.

When he finally asks me to pose that way I am not surprised. It is the place we always have been going. But I am glad he waited—I feel more at ease in front of him now than I did the first time he did the pastel drawing of me fastening my garter, which was me putting on clothes instead of taking them off.

"You can go behind the screen to get undressed if you want," he tells me.

"Why bother?" I say.

So I sit on a chair in front of him and roll down my stockings, and then stand up to take off my dress and stays, my chemise and petticoat. I turn away from him a little, but not much—a quarter turn. In my mind I tell myself it is not so different from taking off my clothes so we can lie down together. We did away with all the romantic fumbling weeks ago, and now we each undress separately, quickly. That is the kind of lovers we are. So that is what I have on my mind when I stand draping my things over the back of the chair: how we are together.

But instead of climbing on top of him on the divan, I say, "Where do you want me?"

"Here," he says, and shows me. And positions the cheval mirror so the light from the window catches my side.

"What do you want me to do?"

"Anything."

"Take down my hair?"

"Yes."

So that is what I do: I stand in front of him and uncoil the bun I have my hair wrapped in. I hold a couple of pins in my hands and then I do what I always do—I put some of the pins in my mouth until I loosen the knot of hair. Then I take all the pins from my mouth and let my hair fall down on my shoulders. No, not fall—hair does not fall. I let my hair slip over my shoulders.

I want to ask him if it is what he wants, but I do not. He would tell me if he did not like the pose, and part of me knows it does not matter what I do. He wants to see me, that is all. I am doing something private and I am letting him watch. It is enough.

My hair feels soft and warm on my neck, but the rest of me feels the air of the studio. That is the thing I notice more than anything: the air on my skin.

"Now put it back up," he tells me after he sketches for a while.

"I need a mirror."

"Do it by feel."

So I reverse the process. I put the pins in my mouth and hold the center of the twist with my left hand and wrap the length of my hair once around with my right. Then I switch hands and hold the twist with my right and wrap with my left. That is how I coil my hair, hand over hand, and when I get the ends tucked under, I slip the first pin in and then the others. At the end I reach around to check the coil, middle fingers and thumbs touching. He cannot see any of it because I am still facing him, but my arms must make a frame for my face because that is when he tells me to stop.

"Just stay like that."

And I wonder what it looks like to him.

I have been thinking about the coil and the pins in my mouth, but with my arms bent like wings behind my head, I think about how my body must look to him now that he is drawing me and not touching me.

"Look at me," he says.

So I do. With my hands still touching my coiled hair, I look toward him and I let every single thing inside me show on my face, on my breasts and belly and legs.

When his eyes meet mine, I feel light-headed and dizzy, and my body starts to heat up the way it did when Nise and I were at Moulin's. But I keep on looking at him, and he must know what I am feeling because just then his whole expression softens. I do not know how else to say it. His eyes change and along with that, his whole face grows kinder.

He does not say anything but he does not have to say anything, and the worst of light-headedness passes. He goes on looking at me, watching me. Making light marks on the page but mostly just watching me. Wanting to make sure.

After a few long moments in the silent room, he begins working steadily again. Turns his full attention to the sketch. Only then does he say, "Ça va?"

"Yes," I say. "I'm here."

⚜

When I go to get the francs from the table by the window, I watch him begin to write in his notebook the way he always does, Victorine Meurent, and the amount he has stacked neatly for me.

"I should use your real name, you know," he says. "For my records."

"That is my real name. Victorine."

"I thought that was made-up. I thought that was your joke."

"It's on my birth certificate," I say.

"Why did you tell me it was made-up?"

"Nobody was telling the truth then," I tell him.

"But I heard Denise call you Louise," he says. "I know I did."

"That's my middle name."

Finally he nods. So there it is, in his notebook: *8 septembre 1862, Victorine Louise Meurent, 25 francs.*

One week's work.

am walking home from his studio, looking in shopwindows, looking at the people, daydreaming, when I smell her.

I mean that seconds before I see someone standing in front of a store window, before I realize the scent comes from her, I smell jasmine. It is heavy enough to waft out into the air behind her. When I realize the perfume comes from her, I pause as I am passing to see what kind of woman would wear such a heavy fragrance. I can only see her from behind, and that is when I notice the sharply cut jacket with the velvet piping, the hat pinned to her hair at just the right angle to show off the massed curls and long earrings.

Only after I take in all that—the jasmine and the velvet and the jet earrings—only then do I see the rash on her neck.

Fingers of red reach down from her hairline and disappear into her collar. When I first see them I think they are birthmarks, taches de vin. But they are not. The rash is raised. Weeping in places.

I look for another long second and then I turn away from the smell of jasmine and the weeping skin. Turn completely away.

Yet even after I move off down the street and go blocks away, I still feel as though I can smell her perfume.

The pieces do not go together. To pin up her hair tightly under a hat instead of keeping it low on her nape, to choose earrings that draw even more attention to the neck. To take that level of care— and then the offended skin. And yet what choice is there? To hide?

Sometimes I saw people with it at Baudon. One of the engravers had a bad case. He was young and good-looking, handsome even. He looked fine until he lifted his hair out of his eyes and then you could see the ulcers on his forehead. Circles and disks. Every day at work people asked him, "How are your 'buttons'?" and they would laugh. He took it, took the constant ribbing and insults, but when he healed, he quit. Moved on.

And why wouldn't he. Why not go someplace where people did not know his business? It is easy enough to disappear in this city.

The engraver was not the worst. Once, when I was about eight years old, I saw a woman with a veil on the street. It was not the airy netting they put on women's hats—I do not mean that. She had the lower half of her face wrapped in a scarf even though it was not cold. When I asked my mother why the woman had a scarf on, she said, "Not now." So when we were a little further down the street, I asked why again.

"She probably doesn't have a nose," my mother said.

Of course I turned around when she said that, to see if I could still see the woman in her veil. I thought I could make out the back of the woman, but I could not see her face. When I tried to recall what I had just seen, I realized I did not remember seeing any lift in the scarf where a nose would have been. That is when I understood what my mother meant. The scarf fell straight from right beneath the woman's eyes.

"She could have got it from her husband," my mother said then, even though I had not asked anything more.

I did not understand what my mother meant, how someone could lose her nose because of her husband, but something about the comment made sense. Because that is what the woman looked like. Ordinary. In a dark dress with a whitish collar. Like my mother. Except she did not look at all like my mother because she had a scarf covering her face. And because above the scarf, her eyebrows were knitted together, as if she were in pain.

Plombée. Poivrée. La grande vérole. La baude. People call it all kinds of things.

I get nearly all the way home before I think about how I did not see the jasmine woman's face.

do not think it is a coincidence that it happens after I start posing naked for him. My nakedness makes everything that much sharper between us. That much keener. Sometimes the air in the studio seems as though it is water, as if I could swim in it. Other times it feels like the air after a rainstorm.

We are coiled together on the divan when it happens, my mouth on him, his mouth on me. I pull away from him so I can make the sound that comes up out of me.

"Is that the first time?" he says when I am done.

"With you, yes," I say. But as soon as the words are out, I hear how they sound, and I say, "I mean it's the first time with a man. There was never time before when I was with someone. It was always rushed."

"But you felt it before," he says.

"By myself. When I touched myself."

Of course he wants to see me touch myself then. He moves the big cheval mirror to the foot of the divan and tilts it a little, and when I look into it, I can see my face, but also my hand on my sex.

He comes to lie beside me then. I can see myself and I can see him, too. I can watch his face as he watches me.

"Now show me," he says. And slips a finger inside to help.

After, when I wake up from napping with him, I look around the studio and then at him sleeping, and something feels different between us. Maybe because of what happened today, maybe because of the posing. I close my eyes, but when I look back at his face again, he is awake. Watching me.

When we begin to touch each other—when I touch him there and have my hand around his cock—I let my one fingertip go to the rough scar at the base. It is not a big spot but the skin is thicker there, paler than the rest. I keep my fingertip there and I look at him.

"Ma cicatrice," he says. "I wondered when you would ask."

"What's it from?"

"A malady. A bad story. When did you notice it?"

"The first time we were together," I say.

"You don't have to worry. It healed long ago. I got it from a very nice woman."

"Nice?"

"Yes," he says. "Let's leave it at that."

I do not tell him the scar frightened me when I first felt it. That I did not feel it until he was about to move into me. That I stayed frightened until after, when I saw the healed skin.

"Did it hurt?" I say instead.

"Like the devil. Along with the treatment."

I want to ask him more about the woman, but I do not. It is his story to tell or not to tell. Still, I cannot help remembering the perfumed woman I saw walking on the street. Whether she was nice or not I cannot say, but she had money and it did not matter. The rash still snaked over her neck.

But it is one thing to have weeping skin and another to have a scar.

So I keep touching him and running my hand over him until he gets hard. I make a point to include the scar. Not to be afraid to touch him there, too.

On Friday we finish for the day and I am in my petticoat, pulling on my boots, when he says, "Are you up for a challenge? This evening?"

I think he means something sexual because he is lying on the divan as he says it, shirt still unbuttoned, watching me dress the way he always does. So I walk over to the divan in my boots and chemise and put my hand flat on his chest.

"What kind of challenge?" I say.

"Come and meet my friends. They say I'm keeping you secret."

"How do your friends even know about me?"

"Tonin has known about you almost from the start. Astruc came the other day and saw the paintings."

"And you told them I'm your new model?"

"I also showed Astruc the pastel of you in your garter. I think he liked your breasts."

So he is not hiding anything from them, which surprises me.

"Do I have to do anything special?"

"Be yourself," he says. "That's all."

He tells me then the café is on Rue des Batignolles, just north of the Place de Clichy. Tells me there is a front room and a back, and that they will all be in the back room sometime after dinner.

I guess I look hesitant because then he says, "I'll be on the lookout for you."

"What do they want exactly?" I say. Because that is how I think of things. People always want something, even when they do not say.

He waits a while before answering. Takes the time to search my face.

"They just want to meet you," he tells me.

And in a little while I nod.

I do not tell him that I am flattered by the invitation, and confused by it.

Not flattered by his friends' request—I do not know them and do not know what they want, really. I mean I am flattered by his willingness to let different parts of his life cross. Yet I also know he hides what he loves, the way he hides the painting of the gypsy girl.

I do not know if it is better to go on being a secret or not. Which is safer for him, and for me.

⚜

When I get to Café Guerbois, I almost do not go in.

There are tables and chairs in the streets, and I do not mind walking among those, but when I look through the glass window, I stop. The front room is almost all white: white counters, white tables, white walls. Gold accents here and there. Even though I put on my new blue dress, I feel funny about walking in.

It is not a place for someone like me.

And I am turning away from the glass front of the café when I see him walking toward me from across the street. He kisses me lightly on each cheek.

"I thought you'd be inside," I say.

"I came out to look for you."

I do not want to tell him that it took me longer to get ready than I planned because I decided to wash my hair, that it is still damp at the back. That even though I have on my best dress I still feel all wrong. It is not just that I want to hide those things from him.

I want to hide them from myself.

But now that he is standing there beside me—now that he has kissed me lightly on my cheeks so I can feel his mustache and smell his cologne—I can feel some of the panic in me subsiding. I glance at one of the café tables there on the street, one where there is a carafe of water so cool that water beads on the outside of it, and in that instant I want nothing more than to go inside and sit with him at a table and drink a glass of cool water. So I do the thing I learned to do when I stand in front of him, naked, or when he asks me to put on one of his silly costumes.

I pretend.

I pretend that it is just the two of us, the way it was on Boule du Temple when we were sweethearts like anyone else. And because I am seventeen and wearing the green boots of a whore, and because I know what passes between him and me when we are alone on the divan or in my room, it becomes real. It becomes real because I believe in it.

I tell myself the inside of me feels as cool and clear as the water in the carafe, and I take that coolness with me when we walk through the doors and into the back room at the Café Guerbois.

※

When we walk toward one table, two men stand up. They each nod and take my hand, and he tells me each of their names.

"We're pleased you came, mademoiselle," the one closest to me says, the one he called Tonin.

"You didn't see Duranty out there, did you?" the one named Astruc asks him.

"No, but I'm sure he'll be by," he says. "You know he lives here."

"It's his turf, isn't it?"

The three of them fall into talking about whatever it was they were saying before, and it is a kindness, I think, when they do that. It makes me relax a little, and even though I listen and nod, I also look around—at the room itself, and at the faces of his friends.

This back room could not be more different from the front. The walls are wood at the bottom and painted brown at the top so that the whole room feels like a warm cave. I can see green-topped billiard tables at the back of the room, and a door opening to a garden. There is enough smoke in the room that the air seems filmy with it in places.

Of his two friends, it is easier to look at the one named Tonin. He is the only one who does not have a beard, and I like being able to see more of his face. Astruc is dark-haired and more energetic, and when I catch his eye, he looks at me directly and intently. Not unkindly—I do not mean that—but almost as if he wants to take me apart and see if I match the girl he saw in the paintings and the pastel.

And yet Astruc is not the only one studying and observing me. Each time my eyes fall on Tonin, he seems to be watching me, but he smiles a little, as if he wanted to encourage me, not examine me. And after a few minutes, I realize I have heard the name before: the night he brought Nise and me the copy of *Journal Pour Tous* with the "Langage des Cheveux" in it, it was his friend Tonin he was going to meet. So then I feel like I know this friend of his, and I smile back a little.

The three of them are talking about a book they read, something about the life of Christ, and I cannot follow all the conversation, but in a little while he says, "I'll give them a Christ if they want a Christ. But it will be a Christ of the people, with dirty feet and a cut in his side. A real Christ."

"No one at the Salon is ready for Christ to be real," Astruc tells him.

"There's only beauty in what's real," he says.

The conversation goes on and I follow as much as I can, but at a pause, his friend Tonin turns to me with his brown eyes and kind mouth.

"Mademoiselle, where did you meet this one? When we ask him, he won't ever say."

For a moment I wonder what answer he wants me to give, and then I remember what he said when I asked him if he wanted me to do anything special: *Be yourself.*

So I say, "We met in the street. In front of a shop of knives."

No one says anything, and for a moment I think I got it wrong. I think I should have lied and said something more elegant. But then I see Tonin glance over at him, so I do, too.

"She's right," he says. "I found her on the street. Un porte-bonheur."

"A redheaded lucky charm," his friend Astruc says, nodding. "It's rich."

I look at Tonin, and something about his eyes tells me to speak, to say whatever it is I have inside me.

So I look from Tonin to Astruc and then at him.

"But I found him, too," I say.

For just a moment no one else is at the table. For a moment it is just him and me. Two lovers. It takes just another moment, and then I see his eyes flash and then go liquid and dark.

Which I know is his pleasure. Because sometimes words are like touch with the pleasure they bring.

I do not know how or why, but I end up telling Tonin all about Baudon and what it takes to burnish silver, and how now sometimes when I am posing, I feel like my hands do not know what to do with themselves. I think I probably would have gone on talking and confiding in him, but then a fourth man approaches the table, and everything stops.

The fourth man greets the others and then takes a chair. He hardly glances at me.

At first I think it must be the Duranty they spoke about before, the one who comes to the Guerbois every day after lunch and after dinner. But something about this man's face does not match the stories they have been telling, and then I hear his greeting to the man: *Cher Baudelaire.*

"We thought you were in the North," Tonin says.

"I was, but you know I can't stay away. Yet when I get back I see nothing has changed in my absence."

And I can tell that he meant to introduce me, that he means to do it, but the man immediately begins talking, and there is no space to make the introduction.

There is something dramatic about the way the new man talks, and something impatient. I keep watching his face to understand more, but while he looks from face to face at the table, he makes a point of not looking at me.

He talks at length about a place called Honfleur, and in a little while I understand it is a place on La Manche. And yet I feel that he does not mean for me to hear any of what he is saying, so I do not know what to do exactly. I do not feel I can go on talking with Tonin privately, the way we were before. So instead I listen to the new man, to *cher Baudelaire* as he holds forth. I listen and find a place on the wall opposite the table to study. When I look over to the green billiard tables, I see Tonin glance at me, and I think I can read something in his eyes, but I keep my face flat.

In the end, he has to break in. Tonin cannot do it, nor Astruc. It is not their place. Only he can do it.

"Baudelaire, I'd like you to meet my new model," he says finally, simply, interrupting the stream of the man's words. "Mademoiselle Victorine Meurent."

And only then does the other one look at me.

He tilts his head down slightly, ever so slightly, and studies me from beneath his brows. And though I know it does not make any sense, the look reminds me of nothing so much as the way my mother would sometimes look at me. With disapproval and curt words ready on her tongue.

Yet the one they call Baudelaire does not say anything. He just looks at me with some kind of challenge. And in that moment I realize he thought I was just some girl working the café, someone one of his friends picked up for the evening as entertainment. That he is annoyed he has to somehow include me.

And I do not know how I know what to do next, but I know.

When we first came inside the café from the street, I knew where he had been sitting because he left his gloves on the table. They are his favorites, thin leather, with three tucks stitched on the back, the yellow color of the center of a daisy. Inside they are stamped: *Gants Boucicaut, Médaille d'Or, Paris 1862.* They smell of smoke and his skin and cloves—I know because I have brought them up to my nose many times. And someplace someplace someplace, the gloves must smell a little of me.

His gloves are soft as skin, are skin, and when I reach over to take one, it feels like I am taking his hand in mine. I pull one glove on, and it goes over my hand easily because it is big. And yet it is still like a second skin, like his skin on mine. I let myself feel it for a moment, and then I pull on the other glove.

The whole thing takes seconds. And then I say to the glowering face, to *cher Baudelaire*, "Pleased to meet you."

And something shifts in his gaze. Something becomes sorrowful in those eyes, and instead of saying something cutting, or just droning on and on, *cher Baudelaire* goes silent.

And then, to break the moment—because it is too much, it is too much to hold his gaze, and to go on being stared at, and it is too much for everyone at the table to watch—Tonin stands to get the waiter to bring another bottle of wine. And in another moment Astruc says, "I thought Duranty would be here by now."

Quickly, everyone latches on to that, to telling stories of Duranty. Only Baudelaire and I are quiet.

And because I am seventeen and wearing the bottle green boots of a whore and a black ribbon at my neck, and because I reached over and took my lover's gloves and pulled his skin onto my own—I know what I see when I turn from *cher Baudelaire* and look around.

I see everything at the table has changed. I see everyone at the table has changed.

And when I look to him, to the one whose skin I just pulled over my own, I see he is watching me.

Because he saw the change, too. He saw the whole table change when I pulled on his gloves.

And I feel safe wearing his yellow leather gloves, with his skin on mine.

❦

He and I do not speak until we are blocks away, and when we do, I am the one who says, "Don't you want to go back to your friends?"

"I see them all the time."

"You see me all the time," I say.

"That's different."

"Baudelaire was away, so you can't have seen him all the time."

"I thought he was still away."

"He thought I was a working girl," I say. "Working the café."

"I wouldn't have subjected you to him if I'd known. Sometimes he needs to be the only voice in the room. And he's cruel about women."

I think back to the painting of the mistress, the one with the flat face and awkward leg. I wonder if Baudelaire is her lover. I wonder and then I know.

"But he can't be cruel all the time," I say. "He loves his broken doll."

He does not say anything to me then, just looks at me sidelong. But at the corner, when we step down into the street, he takes my hand up to his mouth and kisses my fingers. Because

I have given him back his gloves, because I am bare-handed just like I always am.

He kisses my fingers and then pulls me to him, there on the street.

⌁

Later, when we are lying in my bed on La Bruyère, he wraps his hand in my hair and asks, "How did you know to do it?"

"Do what?"

"Put on my gloves like that. It was like watching someone pull on sunlight."

"I didn't know."

"But you did. You did the one thing he couldn't pretend to ignore. It was a conscious gesture."

I do not say anything. I do not know why I did what I did with his gloves. I just knew to do it.

In another moment he tells me, "Tonin likes you very much."

"He's your best friend, isn't he?"

"If a man can have such a thing."

We go on lying there, watching each other in the dark, touching, talking. But as my eyes are getting heavy, I know the answer to his question. It comes to me.

"I didn't know to pull on your gloves," I tell him. "My body knew."

He looks at me after I say that. He looks at me for a long time and I let him. I let him watch me, and I return his gaze until I cannot, until I have to let my eyes close. His hand still in my hair.

The next day after he leaves, I am out walking. I came out to buy some kind of lunch for myself, even though it is nearly four in the afternoon. That is when I see the little white sign in the shopwindow.

BAGUE PORTE-BONHEUR
OR SUR ARGENT CONTRÔLÉ
BIJOU CHARMANT POUR FILLETTES

I remember what he said last night to his friends: *I found her on the street. Un porte-bonheur.* And Astruc saying, *A redheaded lucky charm.*

Then I keep the word *porte-bonheur* in mind the whole time I am walking. And in that way the word itself becomes a kind of charm.

This time when he tells me he does not need me for the day, I do not panic. I go to Raynal's for breakfast but then I come back home. That is the thing, I have a room to come to. I can lie on the bed all day, staring at the ceiling or out the window or at my box of candles. *Veilleuse Universelle, Félix Potin, Paris, Exiger ce Timbre.*

But I do not just lie on the bed to nap. For the first time in a long time I take out my notebook and try to figure out what to draw in the room. The creased sheets? The angle of the beam by the mansard? And then I know: I want to draw the window and what is outside the window. The white sign with black letters on the brick red building, HERBORISTE.

I try to draw it with my pencils but in a little while I know I can only get at part of what I see. Because the sign is not really white but bluish white, and the brick is not just red but brownish purple. And that makes me think of what he always says, that colors are the only thing. That there are no lines in nature, just one color next to another. Une tache à côté de l'autre.

I need color.

So I get a brush and a couple of old tubes of watercolor paint that I took from his trash once, from the can beside the back door of the studio. The brush is a bit stiff and the tubes are crimped and flattened, hardly anything in them, but I like just seeing the smears of color and the names: vert de cadmium, bleu de cobalt. The colors of leaves and flowers.

I work the ruined brush in my fingers until the bristles soften a bit, and I think that is it, that is what I want to try to paint. Flowers. Morning glories. And I think I remember them, I think I can see them in my mind's eye, but when I look back at my sketch from the day I went to Toucy with Nise, I see I had it wrong. The flowers are not round but are made up of five triangles, five tiny panels that make a bell.

So that is what I dab on a sheet of paper from my carnet with the gleanings from the paint tubes and a little water from my pitcher: five-sided flowers and still-closed twists of buds, the twirling tendrils of the vines, leaves that are the shape of a *pique* from a deck of cards.

I would like to try painting other flowers but the truth is I do not know the shape of them. Not really. Not delphiniums for certain, but not even lilacs. When I try to paint a sprig of lilac from memory, it just looks like a tree or an odd bunch of grapes. So while there may not be lines in nature, there are shapes, and to paint something, you have to be able to see it.

That is how I decide the next thing.

The mirror hanging above the dresser is small, but if I prop it at the back of the table, I can see my head and shoulders and a tiny bit of my breasts. I cannot paint the right colors but I can at least paint shapes. So I make my braid a green vine on my shoulder and my face a blank, blue oval. Each shoulder is a rounded blue stain where I push the brush flat, and my neck becomes a blue column.

I make myself the color of a flower.

At the end I cannot say the portrait resembles me because it has no features, but there is something right about the angle of the head and how the hair spills over the shoulder—even if the head is blue, even if the hair is green.

It is still me.

And something about all of it pleases me. Maybe just the colors themselves, and thinking about purple and blue flowers, or maybe it is the quiet way I spent the day, adding drops of water to the dried-up tubes to coax out the last bit of paint. The day reminds me of the quiet times with my mother, with her sitting and sewing and me play-sewing, or, when I was older, truly helping her by basting, ripping seams, or just sweeping up.

When I look at the portrait again, it does not seem strange any longer that I gave myself hair the same color as my boots. That green has been inside me nearly my whole life. And when the pages turn dry and crinkly, I stand them up on the table, propped up against the wall. So I can see all the flowers. So I can see myself.

When he first shows me the canvas he wants to work on, I do not understand. There is already a woman there, already a rough image painted. Someone lies on the divan, propped up on a pillow. Her face is a muddy cloud, and much of her body seems to be an outline. After the first moments of looking, I realize that what I think is an outline is not that at all. It is what is left. There was once paint on the canvas, and it has been taken away.

"What is it?" I say.

"A failed effort. A start with no finish."

I look more closely at the thing, and in spots I can just make out the weave of the canvas.

When he sees me studying the painting, he says, "It's scraped almost all the way down."

But it isn't scraped all the way. Along with the outline of a body, I can still make out details of a face. The light and dark areas of the eyes, the shape of the nose. And a maw where the mouth should be.

"The face was wrong," he tells me now. "Some faces are dead. You saw it yourself."

And I think back to the first day in his studio, the day he showed Nise and me the different nude photographs. There was the pretty one he called Augustine, but there was also the photo of the girl who looked dead. But I never said that to him. I just told him that I thought the girl looked bored.

I go on looking at the remnants of the body and the mess where the face should be, and then I say, "Was she your model? Before?"

"She came for a few sittings."

"So you must have liked her."

"There was no way to know what would happen. Some people go flat in a pose."

Maybe it is his words or hearing his voice and staring at the rawness of the model's mouth—but something happens inside me just then. And I do not say a word to him. I do not do anything but turn away from him and the ruined canvas. In another moment I know I have to get out into the courtyard or onto the street—anywhere away from the scraped-down figure.

I pick the back door leading out into the weedy courtyard because it is closer. And I open it and walk through.

⁓

I should never have attempted that painting,"

He stands somewhere behind me. Neither of us has said anything until now.

"I didn't think she was the right model from the start," he tells me.

"Why did you hire her then?"

"I wanted to start the painting."

"What was so wrong with her face?"

"The shape. The planes of her cheeks. Her expression. Everything."

"What's wrong," I tell him, "is to erase someone like that."

For a moment he does not say anything, and that means something. At least he is thinking about what I said. Considering my words.

"I believe you've misunderstood," he tells me. But he says it quietly. And when I hear that quietness, something in me stills. Whatever in me was alarmed by the wreck of a face and that maw of a mouth—that piece of me stills a little, like an animal.

"It's composition. I scraped away paint," he tells me. "Not her."

I understand—I do. And yet. The other model is there. The remains of her legs and torso and face. It is not my imagination. Yet if I am going to pose for him, if I am to become the woman who replaces the erased figure, I have to find a different way to think.

So I remind myself that I am a modèle de profession. That this is a job and not a courtship.

"Why do you think it will be different with me?" I say.

"It will be different."

Which is possibly a lie. I know if he decides he does not like my face, he can scrape it away, too. He can leave a hole where I once was, just as he did with her. Yet just the way I knew he would come over to Nise and me the first day we met, when she and I stood drawing outside the coutellerie, I know my face will be the one he keeps. I will myself to believe it.

"D'accord," I tell him, and I nod. I nod as much for myself as for him.

I am still not sure I understand the canvas he showed me, or what he wants and does not want, but I do understand one thing: my will. My will to wear the green boots of a whore, to not be like anybody else. To be seen.

I do not want to be erased.

⚘

I thought you wanted to work," I say.

Because for all the trouble he took convincing me about the scraped canvas, when we come back inside the studio, he does not go to the canvas or his sketchpad.

He takes me to the divan instead. He makes me lie down and then he kneels on the floor.

"Everything shows in your face," he tells me. "I can't draw you if you're upset."

So he stays on the floor beside the divan. Opening me.

And for all the fear I felt when I first saw the scraped canvas, I think of it now as a ghost. And like any ghost, I push it from my mind.

I let him open me.

He wants a specific kind of pose, so that is where we begin: by looking at other paintings of naked girls on divans.

He shows me a print of a fancy-looking painting, and an actual painting on a wood panel. The print shows a curvy woman from behind, looking over her shoulder, with a peacock fan in her hand. The other, the real painting, shows a woman from the front with one hand draped over her sex and the other holding some kind of leaves. A silky dog sleeps near her feet.

"Those women don't look real," I tell him. I point to the woman with the silky dog and say, "This one doesn't have a bone in her body."

About the other one, the print of the woman with the peacock fan, I tell him, "Her back is so curved she looks like a snake."

He laughs a little and then shakes his head at me. "That's

Ingres. A classic. And I painted the first one. It's a copy of a Titian."

The names do not mean anything to me, but I feel odd knowing I just said something about one of his paintings. Yet it is not just the painting that seems wrong—it is the woman herself.

"Aren't there any paintings that look like real women look?" I say. "Like your gypsy girl?"

He looks at me for a moment and then goes to his cabinet. When he comes back, he holds something much smaller than the print or the painting he just showed me. It is a photograph, but it is a photograph of a painting. He hands it to me and I look at it for a long time.

"It's a little better," I say. I do not tell him that the breasts look all wrong—too far apart and pointing in different directions—or that the woman's feet are too small. All I say is, "Her body's too long. And she doesn't have a neck."

"It's a photo of a painting by Goya."

Just the way he says it, I can tell I annoyed him, so I say, "Of the three, I think yours is the best."

The woman he painted may not have any bones, but I still like it better than one whose breasts seem cockeyed, or the snake-woman, whose face is so perfect it does not even seem as if it belongs to a woman. It is a statue's face, or a face from a cameo.

"It looks as though her breast is in her armpit," I say, pointing to the place on the snake-woman.

And he laughs at that. Really laughs.

"So that's your opinion of the Odalisque," he says.

"I'm just telling you what I see."

"I don't much care for it, either," he says. "It's dead. It's a masterpiece but it's always been dead. The closest is the Goya, but I don't even want to paint that. Not that I could."

"Why couldn't you paint it?"

"No one should paint like anyone else."

"But you could if you wanted?"

"I don't want to paint the past. Not even Goya's past. Il faut être de son temps."

I know I do not understand all of what he means, but I do understand that he wants to be different from anyone else, that he wants to paint something entirely new. As we stand talking, things begin to feel relaxed again between us, the most relaxed since he showed me the canvas with the scraped-off face.

※

"The thing is, lots of women's breasts are uneven," I say.

He wants to start with sketches, so that is what we are doing. The legs of the model were down in the scraped-off painting, but he tells me to lie on the divan with my right leg bent at the knee. It is the leg closest to him.

"Now touch that knee with your other hand," he says.

So I do. And then I bend my right arm, the one that is closest to him, at the elbow, resting my hand up by my collarbone.

The position feels complicated, as if I am all crossed up, but I understand some of why he wants it: by bending my knee I hide my sex, and by reaching across to touch my own knee, at least my other arm shows. At least I do not look like a one-armed woman.

"What made you think about other women's breasts?" he asks.

"That last painting. Goya. Her breasts are pointing in different directions. They're cockeyed."

"But why say most women's breasts are uneven?"

"My mother sewed for women," I say. "She saw their bodies. She talked about it."

"What about you?"

"My breasts are pretty equal," I say.

I can tell he wants me to say something else, to somehow go on, but I do not say anything else. He has told me he does not like to talk while he is working, but just then, I am the one who wants to stop the conversation. Not because I do not feel like talking—I could. But I do not need to. I feel content not talking.

And something happens then between us, in the middle of the idle talk. I feel connected to him, but there is also something about the silly, flirtatious talk that puts me at ease. I feel not just his desire but his pleasure at my company. As if there is some kind of delight he takes in me, not just in my body but in my thoughts and the things I say. Once I become aware of that, I feel weightless and settled at the same time there on the divan. Even though I am naked, it feels as if something were resting very lightly on me—a sheet covering my legs on a summer night, or a loose cotton chemise on my skin.

And that is what the sketches themselves are like. He draws them all in airy red chalk, with just the hint of my features, or with no face at all. But the blank faces do not bother me the way the erased face on the painting did. The drawings are exactly what they were meant to be: sketches. Yet there is also something perfectly finished about them. I see them and do not want any more.

And even though there is no face in any of the chalk drawings, I see myself perfectly in them. My head and hair, my breasts— even my hands. The pose with my hand resting on the opposite bent knee felt awkward, but the way he has drawn it is simple and straightforward. The hand that rests on my knee looks strong— the fingers and thumb look strong enough to belong to a brunisseuse at Baudon, and yet they are pretty. My other hand is turned in, and though you cannot see the fingers, you know I am playing with the end of a twist of hair.

Which I do not remember doing until I see it. But when I see his drawing, I remember. Remember the feeling of my own hair in my fingertips.

The next day, *after I* am done posing, I watch as he walks back to one of the red chalk drawings. He looks at it for a long moment, and then I see his arm begin to move.

He goes on working when I come to stand behind him, and it takes me just a second to see he is making the shadows of the drawing darker, a deeper red. There is a shadow behind my ankle, one beneath my knee, one behind my shoulder, and one along my wrist. The shadow at my wrist is different from all the others because it is on me, not on the cushions of the divan. So he puts the red chalk along my wrist. On my skin.

I do not know if he notices or not, but as he lays in the deeper color, both of his hands move, even the left hand that is not holding any chalk. The left hand seems to want to help with the drawing, so it moves a little, too.

wear a new dress on Sunday when I go to see my mother. The talk about sewing and women's breasts made me miss something about her, which surprises me. Or maybe I just do not want to spend the afternoon alone.

That I miss my father goes without saying.

When I walk in the door, my father hugs me and touches my hair, the way he always does.

My mother takes me in with her eyes.

She notices the dress—of course she notices the dress. That it is blue instead of gray, that it is made of something other than the cheapest fabric, that there is a bit of lace at the collar. That it is not a dress a brunisseuse could buy.

All of that works itself out in her face in the seconds before she embraces me. But she does not say a word of it. All she says is,

"Go ahead and sit down. You're father's hungry so we have to eat. You know how he is."

So I sit and the three of us eat. My mother and father and me.

⌇

After lunch my father sits in the one comfortable chair there is.

"I have to rest my belly," he says.

I help my mother clear dishes and wash up, and when we are nearly done, she says, "If you have time, I wouldn't mind some help with two dresses. I promised one for tomorrow, and I still have most of the finishing to do. And I have another to get ready to fit."

I look at her for a moment, and she must feel me doing it, because without even looking over at me, she says, "Of course only if you have time."

"I have time," I say.

And in that way we fall into our old Sunday habit of her working as my father sleeps and snores, and me helping with small tasks.

"Would you mind doing the hem on this one?" my mother says, handing me a pale green dress. "It's pinned."

And I know without even asking what she wants: a tiny, anchored blind stitch, which, if you do it right, disappears under the lip of the folded cloth, almost invisible on either side of the fabric. I knot the thread and begin, sewing as quickly as I can, but carefully.

For the first few inches of hem, I do the thing I always have done: I push all thoughts from my mind and just focus on the

194

stitches until my fingers find the rhythm and the spacing. In a little while I can think again, but not for those first minutes. For the first minutes I cannot do anything except sew.

"You never lose the knack, do you," my mother says when she looks over at me from her chair.

"I suppose not."

We do not look at each other as we work, but every few minutes she will say something about someone she is sewing for, or tell me something about my father. And it occurs to me that it is peaceful in a way to be sitting there, but that it is also my mother's way: she does not know what to do if she is not working. She would never be able to sit still in a chair until she fell asleep on a Sunday afternoon.

When I am almost finished with the entire hem, she comes over to the table where I am sitting and looks at the work. She shakes her head at me and before she walks back to her chair, she says, "I believe you do a finer stitch than I do."

"I don't think so," I say. But it is still high praise, coming from her. If you work hard and do good work, you can have my mother's respect.

"I see you have a new dress," she says. "The color suits you."

I look over at her, but she already has her head bent, is already back at her own work. I do not know what to say—I do not know what she wants to hear.

"I'm not at Baudon anymore," I say.

We both go on stitching, not looking at each other, and in a moment my mother says, "No, I guessed as much."

"I'm an assistant now," I say. I know it is a vague thing to say,

MAUREEN GIBBON

but it is true: he sends me out on his errands for paints and pastels, and sometimes just for lunch. And I am not about to say the words *modèle de profession* to my mother.

Besides, there are plenty of things about me my mother does not know about me. I never told my mother about going to Moulin's with Nise, I never told her about the day that blood ran down my legs and dripped into my boots.

But if she has a reaction, she keeps it to herself. Instead of asking a question or saying something disapproving, my mother does not say anything. She just goes on sewing. And in a moment it comes to me.

If I showed up at the door looking poorly, she would have plenty to say. But I am wearing a good dress, and I look well. There is nothing she can say. And I knew that. I knew that when I got dressed this morning to come here.

So when I stand up with the finished hem, when I say, "Well, that's a job well done," I am surprised by what she does choose to say.

"It's pleasant to work with someone here," she tells me.

And in another moment she is taking the pale green dress from me, the hem completed, and handing me the bodice of the dress she has been sewing.

"If you would do one last thing and press these seams open, I'd be grateful," she says.

So I go to the pressing board and move the tip of the iron up and down the tight rows of hand-stitching.

"I don't know what we're going to have for dinner tonight," she tells me then, and her voice sounds fretful. "I don't have time to cook and finish this."

I think about telling her I could stay longer, but I do not. I just nod and go on moving the hot iron, keeping close to the seams.

When he asks me if I will go to Moulin's for photos, I do not say anything at first. Then I say, "Why do you need his prints? I can come here every day. On Sundays, too, if you want."

"It isn't what you think. I need you to model, too," he says. "But the camera bleeds away middle tones. I want to see that effect."

I look away from him and then walk away from the table where we have been standing.

"Is that what you want to do?" I say. "Paint from a photograph?"

"Sometimes it helps," he says. "But if you don't want to go, I understand."

Yet when he says that, I know I will have to go. It is not just that I want to please him, either. If I admit that any of it bothers me, it will be bigger than I am. Or maybe I just want to do whatever I can to make sure I am not the one who is erased.

I know it does not matter why I say what I say, only that I say it. So I tell him, "I'll go if you come with me. To Moulin's."

He nods, and as soon as I see that, I wonder why I hesitated. Something in me feels powerful for having said yes. Because if I can give him the thing he wants, I will be the one who gains.

Because I have something he needs.

⌇

When we get to Moulin's studio, of course I see the same tatty lace spread on the divan. I wonder how many girls with dirty feet have lain down on it since Nise and I were here.

He greets Moulin and they spend a little time talking in their hearty way about this acquaintance and that, but I cannot bring myself to listen. When I step out from behind Moulin's screen in one of the robes he keeps there, Moulin is the one to say, "All right then."

And we start. It feels so awkward to be in front of Moulin with him there that I wonder why I wanted him to come at all. When I drop the robe on a chair and go to lie on the divan, my whole body heats up, and I can feel a little bit of moisture starting right there at my hairline.

"How is your friend?" Moulin asks as he fiddles with the camera. "Wasn't it you who came here with a friend? Pâquerette?"

"She's fine," I say.

And because he can tell I feel uncomfortable around Moulin, he takes over the conversation.

"What are you drawing in your sketchbook these days?" he asks.

"Flowers. My room," I say. "The window in my room."

But my voice sounds strained, and I feel the strain in my throat and it hurts to talk.

"What else?"

But I don't say anything and close my eyes for a few moments.

"Do you need to put your head down?"

When I nod, he says, "Just put your head down then. Rest for a moment."

I turn over on the divan so that my breasts are pressed against the lace coverlet, and I shut my eyes. Shut out the room and Moulin. Shut him out, too.

And that is the first photograph Moulin takes. He takes a picture of me lying on my side and belly with my back to the camera. That is the sound that brings me back from wherever I have gone in my head: the sound of him at his camera.

So I turn around. Let them see me.

"I don't know what to draw next," I say—because I want to hear my own voice and want to be more than just a naked girl on a dirty divan. "What do you think I should draw?"

"Draw anything," he says. "Anything that catches your eye."

"What catches your eye?"

"Everything. Girls who stand in the street sketching. Girls in green boots."

When he says that, I look at him.

"What else do you remember?" I say.

"The way you had your hair pinned. Some of it up and some of it down."

"What else?"

"The night you slipped your hand over my leg at Flicoteaux's."

"What else?"

"Your feet on my shoulders."

He says more private things to me, things that are not meant for others, but Moulin is just a noise behind the camera. He might as well be a shadow.

The two of us talking, that is what Moulin photographs. Even though he does not lie with me on the divan, he is there all the same. His voice is in my head and on my skin, and it is as if he is touching me.

I know because this time I do not go anywhere in my head. I stay right there on the divan with his voice. And once I look at Moulin's camera, I do not turn away.

❦

That night when I go home to La Bruyère, I think again about how I felt when I saw the lace throw on Moulin's divan. How what immediately came to mind was all the other girls with dirty feet who had lain upon it. Shown their asses and breasts or splayed their legs.

They were probably like girls I grew up with, or girls at Baudon.

ANGÉLIQUE BACHERET

MARIE CHENART

CLÉMENTINE DOULCET

VIRGINIE TROCHELLE

HONORINE MORANT

EMILIE NALOT

FRANÇOISE RONDOT

REINE THIBAULT

HONORÉE PONCET

ANASTASIE LOISEL

THÉRÈSE JOLIVET

SUZANNE BLONDEAU

ROSE VALOIS

MARIE LOUISE DARCY

ANNETTE COURTOIS

TOINETTE BONAMI

Girls like me.

A*fter Moulin's, something new begins* to happen when
I take off my clothes and lie down on the divan in his
studio.

When I first started posing naked in front of him, it was still
about pretending, just the way it was at Moulin's. I pretended that
none of it bothered me, and soon enough it did not. Soon enough I
became the thing I saw in his eyes. But now another thing begins
to happen.

I get bigger. In the space I take up, in the way I feel in the air
of the studio. I let myself fill the room.

And if I do it right, I become someone else. Not just the thing
I see in his eyes. Someone bolder, more experienced.

And that is what I always craved—experience. With the boy
I stayed out with all night when I was fifteen, with the man I left
home for, with the long-lashed soldier who held me on his thighs,

who made my tongue sore. Because even as a girl I never believed older people when they said things to warn me. I wanted to be taken out of my level of experience. My depth. Sometimes things happened and they were shocking. Or painful. But that is how I became accustomed. And some things I never became accustomed to. That was the price I had to pay for experience.

There is the body he sees and what I am. I know they are two different things. I understand that. But more and more, I can be anything he likes. Anything I like. A matador, a street singer, a society woman in a pink silk robe. And it is not just costumes and clothing I can change—I can even alter the way my face looks by changing what I think about.

Sometimes I remember his story about the soldiers and seeing the body of the man who sold him sandalwood soap, and my face changes. Or I think about what muguet des bois smells like, or peonies, or even my mother's metal shears, because metal has a smell, too. And my face changes again.

Sometimes I think about how it feels when he is behind me on the divan, how it is deeper than when we lie face to face. I do not know what shows on my face when I think of that, but I know something does. I can feel it.

I can give anything he wants me to give. And anything he wants to take, he can have, because I have more. I always have more.

W/hen he shows me Moulin's photos days later, it takes
a while to recognize my face.

But why would I recognize myself. I do not know what my face
looks like when I am with a man, and that is what Moulin cap-
tured. Me with him. Even though he was not part of the photos,
even though we did not touch at all, he is there all the same.

In one photo I have my head turned to the side a little but I am
still looking toward the camera. My eyes are heavy-lidded, and I
look knowing and patient.

In another photo, I see the beginning of a lazy smile but not
the smile itself.

But it turns out he is not interested in my face.

"I'll work from life for your expression," he tells me. "It's the
shadow and light I want."

In the photos I do not look at all like the serious girl in the portrait he painted of me in my work dress. The only photo that looks anything like that portrait is one that Moulin took of me standing. My back is to the camera and I look sideways over my shoulder, so the photograph shows my face is in profile—the plane of my cheek and my eye from the side. I do not know why a profile should look most like the portrait he painted, but it does. There is something similar about the seriousness of my face in both. And that is the only thing linking the photographs and his painting. They might as well be depictions of different girls.

And yet even as I think that I know it is not right. Of course the photos are me. All of them. Just as the portrait with the blue ribbon and the red chalk sketches are me. Faces change all the time. I am different now, standing there with him at the table in his studio, than I was this morning when I woke up in my room and stared at my blue box of candles.

Different phases of the same person.

Different accounts of me.

Sometimes he works right after we lie together. Sometimes he stands naked, too, working. His cock still slick with me.

On those days the studio feels like the freest place in the world. The whole room is filled with us. With him, with me.

After a few days, when he shows me the ink washes beside the photographs, I understand why he wanted me to go to Moulin's.

When he sketched with red chalk, he pared everything down to shape and line. Now, working from photos, he distills everything down to light and dark. Images made of sepia ink and white paper. Sometimes a bit of charcoal pencil.

In two, he uses a thinner wash of ink to show shadows. Mostly, though, it is the deep brown of the ink versus the white of the paper, and that is all. Dark and light. On those sketches, if I pull back and look a certain way, the ink shapes do not even look like a body. But then my eye takes over and makes a picture of them again. Makes them into me again.

So there I am: a swath of dark ink along one side and under the other arm, a crescent moon of ink for a breast, a line of ink to show the up-and-down indentation of my belly. Ink for hair.

Looking at the new washes I do not know which I like better: the airy, red chalk drawings that I thought were perfect, or the bold inks.

When I tell him that, when I ask him how he will choose which one to use as a guide, he says, "I don't choose. I need it all."

The thing is, as soon as he begins to say it, I know what he is going to say. And understand it without him explaining.

"You never did so many sketches before."

"I think it will be an important painting," he tells me. Then he says, "What else would I be doing with my time anyway?"

And from the sound of that I know he is pleased with the inks. Pleased with himself, and with me.

※

When the knock comes at the studio door, I am lying on the divan, and he is getting ready to begin a new ink sketch. I take my clothing and slip behind the screen he has at the back of the studio, but there is no time for him to tuck away the new work or stow the chalk sketches he has spread over the table and clothes-pinned to a length of cord strung along the wall on the side of the studio.

"You're not still working, are you?" I hear a man's voice say. I know the voice—I heard it the night he introduced me to his friends—and in a moment I am sure it is the one he calls Astruc.

"I certainly can stop by later," the voice says.

"No, it's fine. I was finishing for the day."

I can tell by the way the voices sound that the two of them are standing in the side entryway, a narrow nook of a room, and yet even when he brings Astruc into the studio itself, he keeps him there at the front, where there are wooden chairs and a small table. Still, Astruc must see the state of things, because again he says, "Really. I didn't mean to interrupt. I can come back later."

"Have a glass of wine with Mademoiselle Meurent and me," he says then. "We've both worked hard enough for the day."

And he must gesture to the screen at the back of the room because I hear the voices turn, as if both men had turned their backs to my direction. Not that there is anything to see—the screen blocks off a small recess, which is its own room really. I am changing back where he keeps painting supplies and canvases.

Except I left my boots in the room, there beside the divan, and when I come out a moment later, I am dressed but my hair is down and I am just in my stockings.

He turns first, and only when he nods does Astruc turn.

"I didn't know I was interrupting a working day," he says. "But it's a pleasure to see you, mademoiselle."

"And a pleasure to see you," I say. Then I sit down on the divan and begin to pull on my boots.

Astruc walks over to the chalks hanging from the clothespins and looks for a long time, standing up close, not saying anything. Walks from sketch to sketch and then back again.

"But these are astonishing," I hear him say.

And even though all of the sketches are of me, even though I am naked in each one, and even though I am sitting in the same room as the sketches, not ten meters from him—the comment is not directed at me.

"Ils sont naïfs," Astruc says then. "That's their strength. They're plain and bold."

"I draw what I see."

"Are they studies?"

"Of a sort," he says, shrugging, and that is when I understand he wants to get Astruc away from the sketches. That he is not ready for anyone else to see them, or to talk about the painting he is planning.

"Even I only know what I need to know," I say from the divan, where I am buttoning my boots with the buttonhook he keeps there in the studio.

And I do not know if it is the drawings, or the sound of my voice, or the fact that I am buttoning my boots in front of him, but Astruc seems surprised and then embarrassed. As if he realizes in that moment that I have just been naked in this room, or that I am still getting dressed. And maybe it is something else altogether— I cannot tell. All I know is how he looks.

And he begins apologizing for interrupting. Says he should have known better than to call so early in the day. That if we will forgive him he will be on his way.

"Goodbye, mademoiselle," he tells me, but he is already heading toward the side room and the door.

I am still sitting on the divan, still buttoning my boots, when he and Astruc go out onto the street. And when they are gone for a while, clearly having some kind of conversation, I know it was me who made Astruc nervous. My stockinged-feet presence on the divan, or my chalked- and inked-presence in the sketches—I do not know which.

"What was all of that?" I say when he comes back in.

"Where do I start?" he says, shaking his head. "He thinks I'm doing something groundbreaking. He fears it won't be understood. He thinks you are the most natural woman. He thinks the sketches show that naturalness. He wants to write a poem about you."

I wait a moment and then I say, "How can he write a poem about me? He doesn't know me."

"It doesn't matter. He feels he knows you."

And I sit there. At first I do not know what to think, and then it seems funny to me.

"I think my stockings frightened him," I say.

"I think they went to his head," he tells me. "But I am supposed to give you a message from him."

"What?"

"He said, 'Please tell her Zacharie Astruc said, *Never cut your hair.*' So now you know."

"I think he loves you very much as a friend," I say. "I think he loves you and admires you."

"I think he admires and loves," he says. "But I'm not sure I'm the target."

"All he saw were my feet."

"And the rest," he says, and looks over at the red chalk drawings that are on display.

I do not know if it is jealousy or righteousness or just being egged on by Astruc's words, but he keeps me on the divan a long time after that. Showing me just how well he knows me, pleasing me. Pleasing himself.

He *gives me the bracelet* after I am already on the divan, naked, and when he is about to start work on another set of sketches—the final ones before he paints, he tells me.

"So this is what you want me to wear?" I say.

"Yes, I'm giving it to you."

"To wear for the painting."

"It's for you and I want you to wear it for the painting," he tells me. Only then do I think I understand.

"So it's a gift," I say.

"I'm not very gracious."

"It's not that. I just wasn't sure."

A small oval locket dangles from the bracelet chain. Of course when I open it, I see it's empty.

"My mother had a locket similar to that," he tells me. "She kept a lock of baby hair in it."

"Yours?"

"Mine or my brother's," he says. "By the time we were older she couldn't remember."

"But this isn't her bracelet," I say.

"The mother of my son has that locket."

"With a lock of his hair?"

"With a lock of his hair," he says.

He seems embarrassed then, as if he knew the whole topic was wrong, as if he knew he handled it badly.

So I tell him, "I like it. I think it's pretty."

But when I go to put it on, he stops me.

"Can you wear it on the other arm?"

"Like the girl in your painting? The one without any bones?"

"The copy of Titian?"

"The one with the dog at her feet."

If he is surprised that I remember the detail, he only lets it show for a second.

"Like that," he says.

"You have to help me then," I say. "I can't do the clasp with this hand."

After he closes it for me, he brings my hand up to his mouth and kisses it. I do not tell him that is the hand he kissed the night I fed him cherries, the night he turned my palm into a mouth and kissed the nest of veins in my wrist.

Instead I say, "Do you know that's the first thing someone's given me? Besides my parents and my grandmother and the whore?"

And I can tell that now he is the one who does not know what to say. I did not mean to be sad about it, or make him feel like the bracelet had too much meaning—I just wanted him to know the truth.

After a little while, he tells me, "I'm glad, then."

⌇

He tells me the mother of his son was his piano teacher.

At first I do not understand why he is saying it and then I guess: he tells me as he sketches the locket on my wrist, which is like the family locket that the mother of his son has.

"I was seventeen and she was twenty-one when I began the affair," he says. "Isn't that rich? She got pregnant when I was nineteen. I wanted her because she was nearby. Because she was there."

"You don't mean that. You told me she had a beautiful neck."

"That's how it is when you're seventeen," he tells me. "Maybe it's different for girls."

"It's not so different," I say.

"I didn't think about anything else."

"That you might get her pregnant?"

"That. Or how we were two different kinds of people."

"So that's why you didn't marry her."

"No. I would marry her. I feel obligated to her."

"Then why?"

"It's complicated."

I nod a little but I do not say anything. I want to say, *No, if someone like me has a baby at nineteen, that is complicated. For you it was an inconvenience.* But I do not. I know he means something else.

"People aren't what they appear to be," he says then. "Especially the ones who are supposed to be something. Who think they are something."

"You mean people in society."

"Yes."

"Men like you."

He waits and then says, "Yes, men like me."

I do not know what he thinks I will say next, but I tell him, "Plenty of people aren't what they appear to be. Some women leave their children. They have turning doors at some hospitals. *Les tours.*"

He looks up from the canvas then but I do not tell him anything else. I don't say that was the story Nise told me. That when she found out she was pregnant, she thought she would have the child and leave it. That she walked by La Maternité, practicing what to do.

"So I'm not telling you anything you don't know," he says.

"You were telling me a story."

But the story he tells is like a fable: at seventeen he falls in love with a woman, a piano teacher with a white throat. When he gets her pregnant, he feels bound to her and his infant son. Nise's story was not like that at all. No one felt bound to her. And the day that I bled into my boots, the day that Nise helped me, she was the only one bound to me.

I know one thing. I do not really like any of the stories.

He does not say anything else then, not about the woman who

is so different from him, or about his son, or about lockets with scraps of baby hair.

꧁

All that is still working in me when I walk home that day along Rue de Londres and Berlin and Clichy and Pigalle, when I buy carrot fritters for my dinner, when I stand washing at the basin in my room on La Bruyère, where he shows up often enough that people think he is, if not my boyfriend at least my protector. It is still in me when I lie down to sleep, but it is only when I lie down to sleep that I let myself think of it.

The mother of his son holds a place in his life, and it is a surer one than mine. I understand that. But if he loved her still, I doubt he would talk to me about her. I think it is why I do not feel jealous. In some odd way I feel safe with her. She gets some of his time and I get the rest. I envy her place in his life, the space she takes up in it, but she paid something to get it. She had his son, which is a price I am not willing to pay.

Suzanne. That is her name. He said it once without meaning to and then never said it again. She has her role and I have mine. We are our own family. Suzanne and the son and him and me. Because I am sure she is not stupid. She has to know about me, too. Maybe he has said my name to her, or maybe she just wonders where he is many evenings. A person cannot paint all of the time.

What I do not let myself think about until I am lying down in bed, until I have thought about all the other pieces of this puzzle, is the question I do not yet have the answer to.

What price will I have to pay to stay in his life? And what will I pay it with? The only things I have of any value are one good dress and the locket he gave me.

But as soon as I think that I know it is not true.

The night I ran to catch him at La Maube, the night I made him kiss me, he told me I did not know what it meant. *To be wanted like that,* he said. Which is the way I have always been. I want and want, and I never stop for caution. Never could stop. Not when I stayed out all night when I was fifteen, not when I walked with my soldier until I liked him well enough to sit on the cushion of his thighs, not when I ran to La Maube to catch up to him. It is the only real thing I have to give. When he looks into my face, he must see it there. All hunger, all ache.

Yet it is not just for him. Whatever my body wants, I give her. Bitter things as well as sweet.

At the studio the next day, after I take off my clothes, I go to the table where he stands, preparing paint. I do not wait for him to turn but slip my arms around him from behind and press my cheek to his back.

"What's this, what's this?" he says as he turns, as he takes my arms from his waist.

For a second I think he will stop me. But of course he does not. He just turns and starts to kiss me. That is how easy it is. When I see that, I wonder why I did not try it sooner.

At the divan I push him a little so he is the one to lie down first, so I can climb on top of him. I wear the black ribbon I always wear now, and that is what he reaches up and touches. The knot at my throat and then the ends that trail down between my breasts. I feel so much from him that I think I will be able to do it, I think I will be able to tell him what I feel for him. I lean over him, hide my face beside his so I can whisper. Because if he does not love the mother of his son, who does he love? And I think that if I say it, maybe he will, too.

But I do not tell him I love him.

Instead I say, "J'aime ça, j'aime ça."

He takes me by my shoulders and lifts me a litte so he can see my face. So I can see his.

"I love it, too," he says.

And we stay like that for a while, just watching each other. I feel as if he knows what I almost said, and I feel as if he said it, too.

I reach down then and take him in my hand. I wait a second, and then I'm guiding him. Right into me. Right up into me.

⚭

After that, he paints.

The two of us naked except for my ribbon and bracelet. His cock in its sheath.

M a chère Mademoiselle Meurent—that is how he
introduces me to his friend Stevens, who comes the next
day when we are done working.

"So this is why you've been hiding," Stevens says.

"Not hiding," he says. "Just working."

"What about you, mademoiselle?" Stevens says. "Do you like
working with him?"

"It suits me," I say. "He suits me."

Stevens looks from me to him. He looks down for a second and
then returns Stevens's gaze. Smiles.

"She cuts to the chase," he says.

"She's original," Stevens says, watching me. "I can see that."

"I only paint what's true," he says. "You should know that,
Stevens."

"Is it too much to ask what you're working on?"

"Nothing much."

"Yes, I know," Stevens says. "You monkey about with colors. Quelle connerie." He turns to me then and says, "Does he let you see it?"

"When it's done I get to look."

"You must trust him," Stevens says.

"It's not about trust," he tells Stevens. "There's nothing to see before it's done."

"All right, all right," Stevens says. "No one will look at your work. Now let's go to dinner. And I'm buying, mademoiselle. Not him."

❧

Over dinner they try to include me in the conversation for a while, but soon enough the talk turns to what they really have to say, which is all about painting and a salon and judges. That is what I pick up on. But it is a relief when they leave me out of the conversation because I can just sit there and listen. It is not like when he invited me to the Guerbois and no matter which way I turned, someone was watching me. There are only two of them and they are absorbed in what they say, so this time I am the watcher.

Stevens is older. Dark hair with just a few threads of white at the temples. Big nose. Not handsome but handsome enough. When he listens to a person, he always seems to wait a moment before replying, which is nice. It is calming somehow.

"I don't regret what I said," Stevens tells him now. "I didn't at the time and I don't now."

"You shouldn't. With one hand they give you a medal and with the other they insult you."

"Only Fleury. Only he has the nerve," Stevens says.

"The stupidity. He wants to see you paint classical themes. Empty myths and dusty costumes," he says.

"The jury is not interested in 'La vie moderne,'" Stevens says.

"No, they want what they already know. But I'd rather paint what I see. The here and now."

"I stand behind you," Stevens says. "But it will be a long road, you know."

He only nods. Takes my hand, which he has been holding under the table, and moves it over his thigh, up close to his cock. I do not think he cares if Stevens can see or not—I think it somehow makes him feel better to do that in front of his friend. Or maybe he just wants to be sure of me, I cannot tell. We sit like that, all three of us together, until the food comes.

⌖

After dinner the three of us walk along the boulevard together, he and Stevens and I. Of course I am on his arm, but he gestures to me to take Stevens's arm as well.

So I do. I reach with my free hand into the crook of Stevens's arm. I slip my hand between his arm and his side, and just like that I'm holding him, too. I can tell from Stevens's face that it pleases him. It pleases him to have me touch him, and it pleases him to be walking like that, the three of us, to be joined.

It is curious to be the one in the middle. Of the two men, Stevens is taller, so it feels different walking next to him. I feel sheltered in a different way. But mostly I think that this is what it must have felt like when he went promenading with Nise and me. He had his arms full of us.

I do not hold Stevens as close as I hold him, but I still feel his warmth against my side.

It is like being engulfed. But also like swimming above.

⁂

When we get close to Stevens's place on Rue de Laval, he says goodnight to the two of us.

"Maybe one day Mademoiselle Meurent can pose for me," Stevens says as he holds my hand, as he says goodnight.

"I don't know," I tell him.

"It's a possibility," he tells Stevens. "If you think you're equal to it."

"I might be."

"It's up to her, then," he says.

So I say, "Maybe. Maybe that would be nice."

He gives me a card. It only says his name, Alfred Stevens, but he has handwritten *18 Rue Taitbout* on the card, too.

"My studio address," Stevens says. After I take the card from him, he kisses my hand.

"Surely you can do better than that, Stevens," he says. "Surely her company is worth a kiss on the cheek."

I look at Stevens then, but he does not look embarrassed. He just waits, the way he does when someone says something.

"I don't mind," I say, and step closer to him.

He kisses me very lightly on the cheek, but it is long enough for me to feel his soft mustache. To be close to him for a moment.

Then the three of us really are saying goodnight, there on the street corner. He calls out a final farewell to Stevens after we begin to part.

When we walk away, just he and I, my one arm feels a little lonely. So I say, "How did you ever stand it?"

"Stand what?"

"Losing Nise."

"I gained you," he says.

The words are sweet, I can hear that. But in that moment I realize he does not think of Nise the way I do. He cannot. Because no matter what fantasies he had about the three of us together, no matter how many times he kissed her or had her on his arm or touched her breasts through her dress—he never knew her the way I did. He never shared a bed with her or a basin. He never went hungry with her, was never poor with her, never dreamed beside her. I was the one who did those things. I was not a lover but I was like a lover.

So I was the one who gave her up. It was my loss, not his.

When I realize that, I hold his arm tighter. I hold his arm tighter against the cage of my chest. Which he thinks is romance and desire, which it is in a way, but it is something much plainer, too.

It is need.

I need him.

Not just as a lover but in the ways I used to need Nise. For closeness. So I do not feel lost.

And yet maybe those things are closer than I think. Desire and need. And not just for me. I know what his face looks like sometimes when he is above me, moving into me. If that is not need then I do not know what is.

I think all that with his arm hard against my side. With the bone of his arm against the bone of my arm.

⌒∿⌒

He stays with me that night in the room on La Bruyère and the next morning, I say, "So what are his paintings like?"

"Whose paintings?"

"Your friend. Stevens."

"They're like him. Kind. Romantic."

"It sounds as though you don't like him."

"I like him very much. He's a true person. And a true friend."

"But you don't like his paintings."

"He pleases people," he says. "It's a trick I can't learn."

"I don't think it's so bad to please people," I say.

"If it happens, it's fine. If you set out to do it, it becomes another thing."

"Does he try to make people like his work?"

"Not always. But his paintings have a preciousness. I can't

fathom it. The painting they gave the medal to last year was of a dewy-eyed mother and son."

"Now I want to see for myself," I say.

"You have his card. Go and see him."

"I will sometime."

"You're entirely free."

"Aren't you jealous at all?"

"Why should I be?" he says. "I'm the one who had your hair over my thighs last night. Not him."

He pulls me to him then, and I must be just as crude as he is because whatever he says, I say it back.

Le joujou, le chat, d'un côté.

Le vit, la lance, de l'autre.

am in my room the next day, putting up my hair, when someone knocks on my door. It is a boy I don't know but feel as though I should.

"Monsieur asked me to bring this to you," he says, and he hands me a letter.

Of course it is from him—he is the only one who knows I am here, the only one who would send a boy, the only one who would write a letter.

It is just a short note, and in it he tells me that his father died, that he may be some time dealing with family business, that he will send for me when he can. An apology for his haste. There is no real signature, just an *E* and a squiggle.

"Thank Monsieur for me," I tell the boy. "Please give him my condolences."

"He's already gone," the boy says. "He left as I was leaving."

"When you see him," I say.

After the boy goes and I hear his footsteps disappear down the stairs, I wonder about what it all means for him. I do not know much about his family, but from what he has said about his father, I know whatever relationship existed was strained. But it is still his father, and it is still a loss.

I think about writing a note myself, but I do not know where to send it. Then I think about taking it to the studio, but I doubt he would be there to get it. I also know that part of his reason for sending me word is so that I do not come to the studio.

So that I do not intrude on the other portion of his life.

Any sympathy I have to express will have to wait, it is clear, and as I sit there mulling it all over, feeling for him and feeling at a loss to do anything, a tiny part of my mind goes to one particular detail. One I hate even admitting.

He would have paid me tomorrow for the past week, and while I have money for this week, that is all I have.

I tell myself I have lived on less. I tell myself the room is paid through the end of the month so there is not that fear.

Still. It makes me understand how unsure it all is, and how everything my life now rests on depends on him. And now I have the whole day to think about it. To fret about it.

So I tuck his note back in its envelope and finish doing my hair. I know I have to go out, even if it is just to go walking. Just to get out of the room and away from the envelope addressed to *Mlle Meurent*. His handwriting.

Because a walk is free.

It does not take me long to get there—out the door, up Rue de La Rochefoucauld and Rue Pigalle, and then into the square. Everyone mills around and from a distance, it looks as if it were some kind of street party. Except it is not a party but a market. Instead of flowers or birds or horses, artists can take their pick of women. He told me about the place that first day he hired me. Told me he would be just as glad to hire me as to come here.

I see whores, but I also see girls like the ones I worked with at Baudon. Would-be brunisseuses, paper flower makers, laundresses, waitresses, servants, assistants to hairdressers, clerks and seamstresses. At times the crowd sounds just as rowdy as the workroom at Baudon sounded, but other times everyone seems to go quiet. Waiting. Wanting to be chosen.

I stand not too far from the café Nouvelle Athènes but not so close to it as to be mistaken for a customer at one of the outside tables. Even though I am away from the throng, I can still overhear bits of conversation. I hear one woman tell another that if she does not get a job today, she will run the streets.

I walk away as quickly as I can without drawing attention. I try to walk as if I am just a person on the sidewalk, someone walking to a destination. I try to make my face look as if I have a place in mind and a time to be there.

And though I do not mean to do it, I head up in the direction of his studio. Not to Rue Guyot directly—I know better than to go there. Instead I walk up by Parc de Monceau. It is not until I get there that I understand where I have been coming.

To the cedar tree he likes.

He and I walk this way sometimes, up from the old boulevard Malesherbes, into the new district they are carving. They have taken out old buildings, garden walls, and rises in the land in order to make streets with no houses on them. But for whatever reason they keep the cedar.

"It was in the middle of a ruined garden when I first saw it," he told me the first time he brought me here. "The branches reached out among the ruined flowers and made purple shadows."

The tree is part of what will be a city block, but nothing is built yet. So I just stand there on the dirt for a long while, looking at its blue-green needles.

I think, *I still have money in my pocket.*

I think, *I still have my bloodstone burnisher.*

I think, *I am not adrift.*

And I let myself think of him. Of his grief. Because whatever his father was to him, it is still a death.

And then I go on walking.

This time when I go to Baudon, I do not wait down the block and across the street, past where the soup seller stands. I wait directly opposite the side courtyard, the one where the door to the workshop slides open on a pulley. When all the workers start to flow out of the courtyard and into the street, it takes me only a moment to spot Nise. It takes her a longer time to see me, and in that bit of time I wonder how her face will change when she sees me, whether in anger or something softer and sadder, like when we said goodbye.

But when she does see me, all she does is watch. Take me in. Nothing changes in her face. The only thing that changes is her eyes, and the change is so small that anyone else would miss it. So I am the one who waves, who begins to walk toward her. Because it is what I came to do. Still, when we are within talking distance, she is the one who speaks first.

"Eh, frangine," she says. "Did you come back looking for your old job?"

I don't say anything, just shake my head and go on letting her look at me. But in a moment, I see her lift her chin a fraction, and I know she is waiting for me to answer.

So I say, "Ça va, Nise?" Make my voice as warm as I can.

"It goes."

"Working hard as always, right?"

"Hardly working," she tells me.

It is our old routine, and we look at each other for just a moment longer before falling in with the ribbon of workers making their way down the street to lunch. And it is not until we are walking that I realize there was another emotion I saw in her face just now. Not just anger and impatience, not just a challenge.

Puzzlement. And as soon as I have the word I know it is the only real response to my presence. *Why?*

"I wanted to see how you were," I say. "Let's get soup."

"Suit yourself," she tells me, but she drifts in a little closer to me, the way we used to walk together, shoulders almost touching.

The seller has potato soup today. And even though I do not know when I will get paid again, I do the only thing to do: I stand my friend to a bowl.

We sit on the stoop we always used to sit on. We have the bowls in our hands and do not look at each other, and for a moment it

234

feels the way it used to. For a moment, weeks have not passed since I saw her last. But weeks have passed, nearly two months since I last tried to see her. So after a little bit, I say, "Are you still on Maître-Albert?"

"No."

And when that is all she says, I think it might be all she is going to say, but then I hear her take a breath.

"I'm at Toinette's now."

"Did you go in on a room together?"

"I stay with her at her parents'. With her parents and little brother."

"Is it all right?"

"It's not bad. It's almost like having a family. The grandmother lives there, too. She sleeps in an alcove by the stove."

She waits a second, spooning soup from the bowl, and then she says, "Except it's easier than having a family because I'm not related to any of them."

We both laugh. And even as I am laughing, it hurts me. He and I laugh, we do, but I do not laugh with him the way I did with her. The way I do with her, even now. Even now.

"What's really going on with you?" she asks then, straight out into the air above her bowl, still not looking at me. "Why the hell are you even here?"

I think about different things to say, different ways to say them. "I wanted to see how you are," I tell her in the end. "I miss you."

Yet even as I am saying the words, though they are the truest thing I can say, I know they are also a lie. Because if I could be, I would be in his studio on Rue Guyot. I would be there with him instead of sitting here with her.

I look at the side of her face, which I know almost as well as I know my own. When she turns toward me, though, I do not see the anger I saw before, or impatience, or even puzzlement. I just see tiredness around her eyes.

"Did he leave you? Is that why you're here now?"

"No. Maybe. His father died. He's away. I don't know for how long."

"Do you really think you're anything to him?"

I let the words sink in. She has the right to say them—she knows him, knows the game he played. And she knows me. Above all she knows me.

"I think I'm something to him," I say. "I'm not sure what."

She watches me but does not say anything, and then she looks away from me. But there is nothing for her to say. It is not why I came, anyway—I did not come to talk about him. I came to see her. Whatever else is true, that is true. I came to see her, to sit on a step with her, shoulder to shoulder. To slurp soup.

"I think you're bad luck," Nise says then, still looking out into the air. "I think the only reason you're here is that he's gone."

"I came once before. You were with Toinette. I felt bad about lying to you."

Even from the side, I can see her shaking her head.

"You know, I never wanted him the way you did."

"At the start you did."

"Maybe. But not in the end. Not enough to lie for."

"I didn't want to lie."

"But you did."

"I know," I say. "I'm sorry."

"It doesn't matter," she tells me. "You're not my concern."

The two of us stand, take our empty bowls and spoons back to the marchande. After we hand them over, we begin making our way back to the courtyard.

"That was a stupid thing I said when I first saw you, wasn't it?" Nise says just before we get to Baudon, and this time she does look at me. Even now, I still feel the space forming around me that I always felt when she looked at me. It is what her eyes do to me.

"No, I really thought, *Here's Louise. Maybe she's come to get her old job back.*"

"I'll come back if I have to," I tell her.

"No you won't. You got away once. You're smart enough to stay away. So stay away. We're like smoke. Remember?"

It is what she and I always used to say about ourselves when we were out and about, meeting this one and that, scheming ways to get someone to buy us dinner: we were like smoke, always able to find a way in and a way out.

"You can't come back here anyway," she says then, and nods once at the courtyard. "You aren't the same. You couldn't take the job anymore."

I do not say anything. I do not say anything about how little money I have left, or how just yesterday morning I was looking at my burnisher. I do not even bother to say, *I can take it.*

I hug her instead. She smells of metal, crocus martis suds, and her own scent, which is hair and skin and sweat. She smells the way I used to smell. Holding her, I think of all the times she pulled away from us—from him and me. I think of how I would have gone along with it all if she had permitted it. If she had wanted me, too.

Before she pulls away now, I say, "Je pense fort à toi."

I think she might tell me she misses me, too—I think I can feel that in her—but she does not say anything. Just starts to walk into the Baudon courtyard. But just before she turns in, she looks back over her shoulder.

"I'm at Toinette's. Don't forget," she calls.

And it is like a little light coming in at the bottom of a closed door.

The next day, to forget about breakfast, I go to Rue du Grenier-Saint-Lazare, La Maison du Pastel. He sent me here once with a list of colors, and I always wanted to come back. Today I feel better as soon as I see the yellow sign in the window.

PASTELS POUR ARTISTES

TENDRES

DEMI-DURS

DURS

ÉCOLIER

CONIQUE

The shop itself is filled with hundreds of drawers and wooden trays, all of which hold the pastels. But you do not have to bother anyone to open the drawers in order to see all the colors—they have a display of all their pastels hanging on a wall. Real bâtonnets glued to panels. Pastels in all their nuances at the center, surrounded by four oblong rings of colors, with the slenderest bâtonnets on the inside and the largest coniques on the outside.

That is the thing about pastels: the color is not hidden away inside a tube like paint is. So I am able to see:

> the color of paving stones
> the color of my room at midnight and at five in the
>   morning
> the blue of morning glories and the blue of
>   delphiniums, as well as the greens of their leaves
> the blue-green of his cedar
> the bright red of the cherries he painted for the boy
>   and the somber red of the cherries he painted for
>   me
> the color of coffee and then coffee with milk
> the green of my boots
> the color of clouds, which is not gray or blue but pale
>   green
> the pale gold of the sponges
> the blackberry of his vest
> the color of my own hair

Standing there, I think if I were going to buy colors to really use, I would need a variety—a rainbow or a bouquet. But the way the pastels seem prettiest to me is the way the shop has them arranged, color by color, with all shades side by side. You can see what black does to a color, and also white. And I know from the day I picked up bâtonnets for him that they have all the variations of a color arranged in a single drawer, in columns and rows, with the darkest at the bottom left and the lightest at the top. As if the colors were families, with the brooding ones on the bottom and the bright happy ones on top.

When the man behind the counter asks me if I have brought a list today for Monsieur, I shake my head no.

"No list today. I just wanted to see the colors," I say, and he nods. He nods as if it is the most normal thing in the world, that someone like me—a girl with no money, in a mended dress— would come just to see his colors.

I turn to leave the store, but just as my eyes sweep over the trays one last time, I see a small wooden box on the counter, opened to show the pastels inside. When I step closer, I see they are all blues. Seven bâtonnets, seven shades of one blue family, all in a box that could fit in my palm.

"Bleu outremer," the man tells me when he sees me looking.

As soon as I hear the name it makes me think of his box of pastels, which is nothing fine. No brass clasp on the box, and none of the bâtonnets have any paper left on them. They are broken and in pieces, some worn down to nub ends. In that shabby box he has not only shades of bleu outremer but also carmin, vert pomme, violet iris, jaune orangé brillant, rouge capucine, cadmium orangé, jaune d'or and vert forêt. Those were the colors he wanted to replenish, that he wrote down on the list he sent me to buy that day—the list I saved and tucked in the back of my sketchbook.

I do not say anything. I stand there and nod, trying to fix all of it in my mind. Not just the variety of blues, but the way they look in the box. Like tiny birds or jewels or flowers, I do not know which.

That is the picture I carry in my mind when I walk away. I do not feel hungry or scared when I think of those blues in a small brass-clasped box. Bits of sky that could fit in my hand.

From *Rue du Grenier-Saint-Lazare* I walk over to Rue Rambuteau, heading toward Rue Pirouette. I see the people around the marchande before I see her there on the trottoir, underneath an awning. She sits with four kettles around her and dishes up from the kettle right in front of her, the only one with the lid off. For ten sous you get a small piece of bread and a ladle of soup.

Still soupe du matin but so late that I get the bottom of the pot where the creamy broth has thickened with chunks of cabbage and leeks. At first I smelled the soup, so blindingly cabbage that it perfumed the air for a block, but now that I am standing here, eating, I cannot smell it. Can only feel the fullness in my mouth and the warmth going down.

Three workers in their aprons and caps stand there with me, slurping.

When I'm done, I hand my bowl to the old man sitting beside the marchande, who has been steadily washing bowls and spoons in a wooden bucket. I finish before any of the workmen.

The first meal of the day, and maybe the last. I should have taken my time eating it. Should have been more like the workmen, who did not eat as quickly as I did for fear of leaving most of their soup on their mustaches.

When *I get back to* my room La Dame Gaillard says someone came by to see me.

"Not Monsieur. Another man," she says, and watches me.

"Did he leave a message?" I say, keeping my voice flat.

She does not saying anything but hands me a letter, one written on heavy paper in handwriting I think I recognize but cannot place. I do not know what to think, but I do not let anything show on my face. Do not open the envelope until I get to my room.

The letter is from Alfred Stevens.

Who has been asked to come by, who prepared this letter in case I was gone, who has been told I may be short on funds, who is glad to be trusted so much by his friend and, he hopes, by me— and who will, if I permit him, pay me my salary if I will be so kind as to come to his studio the following day.

Who is graciously mine.

The letter is so polite it does not seem real, but it is real, along with the repeated address of his studio on 18 Rue Taitbout, and another of his cards. I am so relieved after reading about the promised money that I feel light-headed. Then I think, no, I am light-headed because all I had to eat today was soup on the street because I thought I would do best to get by on lunch and dinner if it turned out I had to make my money last longer.

The letter banishes all those fears. Even though it is from Stevens, of course it is from him. And after I am done feeling woozy, that is what I think: whatever it is he is going through, he managed to think of me in the midst of it. And that matters as much as the promise of money. Even in my hunger I know that.

I put the letter away and take myself out to Raynal's. For a second I think about ordering a chop but do not—it is best if I keep close to the seam until I see the money in my hand. Besides, I think I would shock le maître if I ordered anything other than soup.

Shock myself as well.

❧

Stevens's studio on Rue Taitbout is nothing like Rue Guyot.

For one thing, the studio is clean in a way Rue Guyot is not. There is no old pail beside the back door for trash, no rickety cupboard in the corner for wine, a loaf of bread and mismatched dishes. This studio is a regular *place*, with real furniture—not only the required divan but also plush sitting chairs, a fancy mirror on the wall, a table beside the door where visitors leave cards.

So Stevens is wealthy. But he is an entirely different kind of man, too.

As soon as I come in, he gives me a sealed envelope with money in it, "to put your mind at ease." I do not know how much is in the envelope but it is heavy, and it takes me by surprise. I set it on the table beside the door with my shawl, and then he walks me through the room, showing me this thing and that: tiny, pretty knickknacks here and there, and some of the paintings on the walls. I know he would listen to anything I said—does listen when I say, *how pretty*—but I do not know what to say, so he has to do all the talking, and what he says is so filled with pleasantries I do not know what to latch on to.

And I do not know what to latch on to in his paintings. They are almost all portraits, almost all women, and everyone looks kind and dreamy. Even the one painting that shows some women crying together on a sofa seems pretty. Which does not make sense to me because if someone is weeping it should not be so attractive. So stylish. And if I take a step backwards and consider all the paintings, it seems as though everyone has their heads tilted at an angle. No one looks at you straight on, and if they do, their faces are hopeful, or amused over nothing, or rapt.

No one in the paintings is plain or ugly. No one looks like they work at Baudon.

And I remember what he said about Stevens's paintings, how he told me Stevens tried to please people. But even the people in the paintings want to please. In just a little while of being in the rich, nice room, I feel odd and out of place.

"Perhaps one day you'll do me the favor of sitting for a sketch or two," Stevens tells me now.

"I'm sure I can sometime," I say, but even as I am saying the words they feel false, as if they are not my words at all.

"Quand vous voulez, où vous voulez," he says. "Comme vous voulez."

He walks me to the table by the door then, helps me on with my shawl that I do not need any help with, and hands the envelope with the money in it to me for a second time.

"He was worried about you," Stevens tells me. "You mean a great deal to him."

"I worried about him, too," I say. "He means a great deal to me."

"I'm sure he'll be in touch soon. He can't stay away from his work for long."

"I hope that's true," I say.

He kisses me then, once on each cheek, and in the moment when we are close like that, I kiss him, too. Except I kiss him on the lips. Lightly.

When he steps back, I can see in his eyes that I surprised him, which is what I wanted to do. He cannot help how he talks and how polite he is. But I know—I feel—that whatever kindness he shows me is genuine. Under all the graciousness I sense something real.

"Thank you for being his friend and mine," I say. At first the words sound odd to me, more like Stevens than me. But they are my words and I mean them.

He bows then. He really does. And then I do not feel odd about the money or what I just said to him or what I think about his paintings. I understand something about him. Exactly what, I cannot say, but something.

We say goodbye.

It is not until I get back to my room on La Bruyère and open the envelope that I see it contains fifty francs, not the usual twenty-five I get each week. I do not know whether the money came from Stevens or him, but I think about the way Stevens said *Quand vous voulez, où vous voulez. Comme vous voulez.* How his face looked.

I cannot know for certain where the money came from, and it does not matter anyway. The only thing that matters is that I make it last.

Chère Victorine,

*I hope you are well and taking care of yourself. Stevens said
you came to see him, which is a relief. I have two more days
of family business and then I should be free. If it is fine by you,
I will come to see you in your little room. I want to rest on
your bed.*

E~

That is the note he sends. Not a word about his father's death,
not a word about his loss. But it is not even the words that matter
so much but what he draws on the page, which is a sheet of paper
out of his carnet.

On the bottom, beneath his initial, he has drawn two figures,
a man and a woman on a divan. You can only see her from behind,
her back and ass. She is on top, on her knees, leaning over a little,

riding the man. He has his hands on her ass cheeks, and because she is leaning forward a little, you can see where he goes up into her. The base of his cock rises up into her.

Her hair is coiled the way mine is, and you can see a bit of his beard as he lies back on the divan. But I really know it is the two of us because he has made the bottom of my feet dirty and placed a crosshatched little scar on his cock as it rises up into me.

When he comes to my room he does exactly what he said he would do: he lies down in his shirt and pants on my bed.

"I need to sleep," he says.

"Sleep," I say.

"Lie down in your chemise next to me."

So I get undressed and lie beside him. I think I will not sleep but I do. And I do not know how long we sleep, but I wake up when I hear him shifting on the bed.

"Can you go and get us something to eat?" he says.

So I get up and put on my stays and my dress. When I am putting on my boots he gestures to the pile of coins he pulled from his pockets before he lay down. "Take some money," he says.

"I don't need it," I say. "You paid me."

"Don't be silly. Take it."

So I take his money, and I go out and buy bread and cheese and wine and an apple tart.

But when I get back, he is not lying on my bed, resting. He stands at the table, my watercolor pictures spread out in front of him. The messy morning glories and the blobs of lilacs. My blue-skinned portrait.

He has to look back over his shoulder to see me, and he stays like that for a long time. Bare-chested, in just his pants, holding the portrait and looking at me.

Which I let him do for a moment, and then I come all the way into the room with the basket of food.

"Would you ever have shown these to me?" he asks.

"Why would I?"

"Where did the colors come from?"

"They were old tubes," I say. "You already had them in the trash."

"No. Where did you get the idea for the colors?"

And I know what he means, I do, but the answer is too simple, so at first I think I should keep it to myself.

But I am tired of keeping things to myself.

"They were the colors I had," I say. "So I used them. And I painted the thing I could see. Which was me. In the mirror."

"That?" he says, and nods at the small mirror I still have propped on the table.

I nod. But he does not say anything. Just goes on looking at the paper, at my blue skin and green hair. And in another moment he touches something on the paper.

"How did you know to do this?"

When I go and stand beside him, I see what his finger is touching. My blue shoulder, which is a circle on top of the cylinder that is my arm, a circle at the end of the cross of my collarbone. My breasts are two more circles, my belly an egg.

"Because some of your sketches are like that," I say. "People's heads are circles and their arms are tubes. That's what it looks like to me."

He holds the portrait a moment longer, and then he props it with the others against the wall, there on the tabletop. Then he takes the basket from my hand and puts it on the table.

"I'll get you real watercolor paints," he says. "If you want them."

And the whole thing is so kind I cannot stand it. He is so kind I cannot stand it.

So I do not answer. Instead I start taking the food out of the basket and setting the table. But when I pull the tart out of the basket, I look at him and say, "I don't want new tubes. Just half-used ones. I want to be able to ruin them. I want things you don't want any more. But maybe the right kind of paper."

And then I look away. Because even to me my voice sounds funny, tight and tinny.

But it is not just the offer of the paint that upsets me. It is everything. The past days of him being away, of not having a place to go. The worrying over money. All of it.

I give him credit: he does not say anything else. Does not make me say anything else about my blue and green paintings. Does not ask me what I want.

He just sits down on the bed and I sit on the chair. And we begin to eat.

❧

Only when we are done with nearly all of the bread do I finally get to tell him I am sorry his father died.

"He had a stroke years ago. He was partially paralyzed," he says. "It was a blessing."

"Still."

"Yes, still," he says.

There is something in his voice that lets me know he does not want me to say anything else about it. Or maybe the two of us are just better at being silent together in a room than talking. It is what we are used to. But in a little while, he tells me, "I'm glad you went to see Stevens. I worried about you."

"It was fine," I say.

"He asked me again if you'd sit for him."

"Maybe," I say. "Maybe after you finish what you're working on."

"You won't be free then, either. I have plans for something new. Another nude."

"Like this one?"

"Different. Seated, with other figures. Two women, two men. Une partie carrée."

"We're all nude? The four of us?"

"Just you."

I want to say it sounds a little like him and Nise and me, but I do not want to talk about who the second man might be. Before I can say anything, though, he says, "Now, tell me if you liked the drawing I sent you."

"I liked it."

He brushes the crumbs from his beard and then reaches for me. Pulls me to him.

"Good," he says, and then he asks me what I want done, and how, and where.

The words are so similar to what Stevens said the other day in his studio that I wonder if they have talked. I wonder and then decide I do not care.

And I tell him what I want.

n the end he decides my knee has to come down.

All the sketches he has done so far feature a reclining woman with one leg bent at the knee.

Now he says it is wrong.

"It's too coy," he tells me. "Either it's a nude or it's not."

So he has me extend both legs straight out on the divan. Cross the back ankle over the front. And without even thinking, I slip my one hand over the V between my thighs.

"No," he tells me. "You can't make a shield of your hand. Let me see each of your fingers."

"Aren't I supposed to be hiding it?" I say.

"No. As soon as you put your hand there it calls attention."

"And that's what you want? To call attention?"

"That's what I want. As if you're about to touch yourself."

So I move my hand again. But because I know if he wants it to look real, I need to go to that place. I slip my fingers down and touch myself, but I never stop looking at him, and he never stops looking at me.

In a little while I say, "Now someone interrupts me. Someone stops me."

And I move my hand the last time. Away from the wetness but my hand still there. I do not know what kind of shape my fingers take against my thigh, but at least it is real. At least the real thing shows on my face.

"Ça y est," he says.

And I hold the pose.

❧

I am nearly dressed when he tells me the thing is finished.

"It's time to walk away," he says, and stands back, looking. "Not a single brushstroke more."

When I hear that, I think I will get to see it. I think I will finish buttoning my boots and will walk over to the canvas and see it from the other side, the side that has been hidden from me.

And even though I do not say anything, he must feel it from me because he tells me, "The next time you come, I'll show it to you. Je te promets."

I know there is no point asking then.

"And I won't need you tomorrow," he says. "I'm sure you'll be glad for a day to yourself."

It is the polite thing, I know, to tell me how I will benefit from a day off. But polite or not, he is still the one who decides if I can look or not, who can send me away for a day.

So I say, "You're the one who looks tired. Are you going to rest?"

"Maybe. I wish I could sleep. But I can't turn off my mind right now."

And that is when I know that tomorrow he will not be at home sleeping or resting, or even having lunch with his son and the mother of his son. He will be here, studying the canvas, walking away from it and walking back to it. Which he often does even when I am here. But tomorrow he will be free to do it as much as he pleases with no one watching.

Yet why shouldn't he? The painting is his. It is of me, but it belongs to him. Not just because the whole studio belongs to him—because it is his work. He is the one who agonizes over it, who cannot sleep because of it. And while I am still thinking that, thinking of what all of it means to him, he says the next thing, which breaks me out of my thoughts.

"You can go and see Stevens if you like," he tells me. "You could sit for him. He'd be grateful."

I wait a moment and then I say, "Why? Why would he be grateful?"

"I think he needs something to jolt him."

"Why does he need to be jolted?"

"You could bring him down from that shelf of politeness where he lives."

I look at him but he does not see. He is cleaning up for the day and does not see me looking, and he does not see me shake my head.

"C'est drôle," I say. And when he still does not look up at me, I say, "Tu sais? C'est drôle."

"What's funny?"

"All of it."

"All of what?"

"He's your friend but you talk about him like he's a corpse," I say. "You tell me I have the day off, but you also fill it for me. C'est drôle."

I look at him for a moment to make sure he is watching me, and when I see that he is, I look away. He can be the one to read my face this time. He can look for subtle changes, hidden signs. Or maybe I look away because I do not want to read his face. I do not know why he wants to send me to sit for Stevens, or what he thinks I could do for his friend.

"You can go see Stevens or not," he says. "It's entirely your choice."

"Is it?"

"Of course it is."

I wonder then if he feels responsible for me. Maybe he knows I am sometimes at loose ends when I do not come to sit for him. Maybe he does not want to be the only one responsible for me. Perhaps that is why he wants to send me to his friend: so he is not the only one I depend on.

All I know is his words make me feel odd. I do not know if they are a suggestion or a request. Or more.

"Just for the day, though," he tells me. "You know I have plans for you."

When he says that I search his face for other clues, but I see nothing—nothing except affection and tiredness. So I push my thoughts away. Do my best to take his words at their face value. I can go and see Stevens. I am free to go if I like.

Still, when we kiss goodbye, there is the slight veil between us that is sometimes there. It disappears when we lie together, or when he is drawing or painting me, or when we are in my room together or out walking on the boulevards. It was gone just this afternoon when I lay with my hand spanning my sex, my fingers damp with my own wetness.

But it is here now between us, and it is like the filmy panels Moulin had on the roof panes in his studio that let light through but blocked it, too. The veil is here between us because of the talk about Stevens, but also because we are saying goodbye. Because he has already moved on to the next part of his day. Because he is lost in thought about the painting and other pieces of his life I do not know about.

Yet I know there is a part of me that I keep separate from him, too. And just now when he told me, *You could go and see Stevens,* I closed off a part of myself. Because I did not understand what his words meant. Because it seemed he wanted to loan me to his friend. And I shut myself down. I shut a part of myself down.

So the veil is there because of me, too.

When I walk home I turn all of it over in my mind, and then I tell myself to stop. I can decide tomorrow about going to see Stevens. I do not have to decide today what his words meant, or what I am willing for them to mean.

Instead I tell myself to think about how I do not know what it means to care about a thing as much as he cares about what he does in his studio. I know what it is to love people, but I do not know what it means to love a thing that way.

He has told me I am his best model, son modèle de prédilection, but I know he says it because I am the thing he wants to paint, not because he cares about me. If he painted only what he cared about, he would paint the mother of his son, to whom he feels bound, or his son, whom he loves. And maybe he does paint them. But if care is measured in time, he cares as much about what happens in his studio as he cares about the mother of his son and his son. And that is the thing that I cannot get inside: what it must be like to love something—a thing—so much.

I did not love what I did at Baudon. I liked parts of it, and I was good enough at it, but that was all. And my father, a ciseleur with his own tools, was always content to be at home with my mother, or drinking with his friends. He did not go around thinking about his job when he was away from it. And my mother sewed because she could, because it was the one thing she knew she could earn money doing.

It is not until I turn onto Rue de Clichy and see the sky-blue Imprimerie sign painted on the side of the building that I realize there is one thing that I love. Not a person but a *thing.*

I love colors.

The blue of my dress, the green of my boots, the purple and greens of flowers and leaves—even the black of the ribbon I stole from his studio.

Maybe I do not know what it is like to care about something as much as he does, but I do know something. When I fall in love with a color, I see it everywhere, and I cannot stop thinking about it. I think about the color so much that not only can I see it almost everywhere I look, but I also carry the idea of the color in my mind and think about it even when I do not see it anywhere.

Right now I am in love with the deep pinkish-red of beets, which is also the color of raspberries but not the red of strawberries.

It is the color of some jams, the stone in his tie pin, and the sign for Maison Idoux, Magasin de Vins, on Rue Blanche.

It is violet fuchsia at Maison du Pastel, the deepest color of that family of bâtonnets.

And for a moment I think it is another thing he has given me, this love of color. He talks about it so much—the importance of one color next to another, or how a painting can need a certain hue, and it does not matter if it comes in the form of a glove or a shawl, as long as it is there.

And then I think no, that is all wrong. He did not give me colors or the love of color. They were part of me before I ever met him.

In the scraps of fabrics and ribbons my mother had lying about from her sewing. In the dresses and coats of La Belle Normande. In the morning glories Nise's mother grew up strings outside her kitchen window. Even in the labels of boxes of candles when Nise and I lived in our tiny room on Maître-Albert. In my green boots and copper scarf from the whore, which I loved because they were gifts, and no one had ever given me any before, but which I mostly loved because they were colors. Verte émeraude et cuivré.

Maybe he gave me the words for colors and the reasons for the importance of colors, and maybe he even made me aware of my love. But he was not the first to give me colors. They were in me all along.

When I wake up in the morning, I think for a moment about taking my carnet and going somewhere to sketch. But I do take my carnet with me because of course I know where I am going.

To Rue Taitbout.

When I get there, though, I do not go directly up to the door of number 18—I walk past.

The truth is it was just a short walk down here from my room on La Bruyère. The truth is I get here so quickly I do not have enough time to think or get ready in my mind. So I walk all the way down to Boulevard des Italiens and then up Rue Laffitte and over Rue de la Victoire.

Because even though he told me to go and see Stevens, something about it confuses me. It seems wrong. Disloyal somehow. But as I am walking on Rue de la Victoire, something comes to me.

I am a modèle de profession, and that is my profession: to pose for artists.

I do not know exactly why he sent me to his friend, or what he thinks I can do to jolt Stevens, but it does not matter. He told me I could go and see Stevens if I liked, and I am free to choose to do so.

So I walk back to Rue Taitbout because I choose to. I choose to go to the studio of the painter Alfred Stevens.

⌁

I do not know who is more nervous, Stevens or me.

He greets me graciously, even warmly, but I can see from his face he has no idea why I am there. And that is when I realize he did not talk to Stevens about it beforehand, that it really was just an idea he proposed yesterday. Not a request at all.

When it comes time to tell Stevens why I am there, all the words I think of seem awkward. So I just decide to say things plainly.

"He told me I might come and see you today," I say. "I have the day free."

"That's kind of both you and him."

"I'd be happy to sit for you if you like."

"Right now?"

"If you'd like," I say. "Or maybe some other day."

Stevens watches me for just a moment—but just for a moment.

"No, I'd like to do some sketches, Mademoiselle Meurent," he tells me. "But only if you have time."

"I have time. Where would you like me to be?"

"That chair would be fine."

So I walk to the chair he shows me, one with a straight back and red velvet cushion. I put my bag on the floor beside the chair and then I begin to do my job.

I sit down.

&

I do not know how much time passes, but I do know time is not the same with Stevens as it is with him. I do not go places in my mind—I just try to make my mind a blank. But I cannot help but think that the whole experience of sitting in front of someone I do not know is entirely different from anything I did with him, who was my lover before he sketched me, who knew my body before he ever painted me.

And only when I let myself think that do I understand another lesson of the day. A modèle de profession poses for strangers, not for lovers. Or maybe she poses for lovers, too, but not always. He and I are the exception, not what I am doing here with Stevens.

When I understand that I begin to relax. Let myself settle into the deep part of the chair, hold my back straight and let my shoulders down. And something must change in my posture or expression because I hear Stevens turn over a page.

&

After some time I say, "Would you like me to do something? Take a specific pose?"

"What does he like you to do?" Stevens asks.

I think about telling him the first drawing he ever did of me showed me fastening a garter. That he sketches page after page of my breasts. That sometimes he has me sit on his work table and takes a low stool in front of me and draws my thighs and my sex.

"He likes to draw me taking down my hair or pinning it up," I say instead.

"Do that then. That would be fine."

So I slowly take the pins and keep my arms in place for a long time. I hear his pencil against the paper, and when I think I hear it stop, I take my hands away and let my hair slip down on my neck and look off in a different direction. When I hear the scratching stop again, I bring sections of my hair forward to lie on my shoulders and I shift on the chair so my shoulders and breasts have a different angle.

I do it all slowly and methodically, but I do not know if he has chosen one of the steps to sketch, or all.

But it does not matter. My job is to pose, not to pick and choose.

❧

When Stevens asks me if I would stand up, I say, "Certainly."

I look off in the direction he tells me, and I hear his pencil for a long time. And it is partly that sound and partly the fact that I find it easier to stand than sit, but for the first time since I walked in the door I can feel my mind begin to wander, the way it does when I pose for him.

For some reason I think of my father, of a day when he took

me with him to gather snails at the barrier walls. His face looked so different that day. Relaxed, his eyes at ease. And then I think about how seldom you really know what a person looks like. You just see people's faces fleetingly.

Because we are all always turning away.

I know what the faces of my parents look like, and I knew Nise's face, and now I know what he looks like.

He knows what I look like, too.

One day he had me squat on the table, right there in front of him. Up on the balls of my feet, my arms behind me, bracing me, holding me up. The position so strained I could barely hold it.

I thought it was my sex he wanted to draw. Because he did it before, and he was right there between my legs. Because he drew for a while and then said to me, "Tell me to kiss it." So that is what I thought it was all about.

But instead he drew my face. From that angle, looking down at him. My strained and greedy face.

All that goes through my mind as I stand there, in front of Stevens.

⟿

"Can you change your position again, mademoiselle?" Stevens says.

And brings me back to myself.

I have to think for a moment, but I do the next thing without hesitating. Somewhere inside myself I have been deciding, and now in this moment it is decided.

I unbutton the top part of my dress. I unbutton enough buttons so I can shrug out of it, so my shoulders can be bare.

I am still in my chemise and stays, but my shoulders are bare, and my breastbone and neck. And I put my hands at my hips and turn my head to the right and push my shoulder blades together, the way I would sometimes at Baudon, after I had been burnishing for hours.

And I can feel the heat beginning at my hairline and my nape, the way it always does.

So I talk, just to hear my voice. Without looking at Stevens, I tell him, "This is how I used to stretch on my old job. I'm right-handed, so I never got to turn my head to the right."

He does not answer, but in a moment, I hear his pencil on the paper. I hear him, and I go on hearing him for a long time. I hear him until the heat at my face and my neck begins to disappear. Yet even when I no longer hear him I do not break the pose.

I let Stevens go on looking.

When we say goodbye at the door of course I am dressed again, and it is the same politeness as always. And then Stevens says, "Now, the wage for your time. I know what I usually pay my models, but I don't want to be out of line. Will you tell me what Manet pays so I may match it?"

The question surprises me. Stevens paid me when he was away, dealing with the death of his father, but maybe he did not know what exactly the sum was for. And again, I understand that he and Stevens did not discuss things in advance. When he told me yesterday that I should come and sit for Stevens, it was only a suggestion. Not a request, not an assignment. Not a loan of my services.

None of the things I thought.

It really was my choice to come or not. Now I see it. And for a moment I think about saying the first words that come to my mind, *No, not today. Today was meant to be a gift.* And then I do not say them.

"He pays me by the week," I say instead. "So five francs would be my daily wage."

"I pay my models ten per session. I won't give you less."

He does not pull the money from his pocket but instead walks to the small desk at the side of the room. When he comes he puts a small envelope into my hand.

"Thank you," I say. "That's generous."

I look at Stevens as I say it. I can see he is not handsome. But the expression in his eyes is a pool I can step into.

Which Stevens lets me do.

"Then thank you, mademoiselle," he tells me. "For the gift of your time and your beauty. I hope you'll sit for me again soon."

He bows then, just the way he did last time I was here, but this time it does not feel so odd. And when he takes my free hand to kiss it, I let him.

Then I walk out onto Rue Taitbout.

It is not until I am close to La Bruyère that I think I understand why I did it.

Stevens did not ask me to undress—I was the one who wanted to show him my shoulders and throat, the bone on my chest where my breasts begin. I wanted to do it even if it was hard. I wanted to do it for the same reason I did things when I was younger. Because I craved the experience. Because if I could do it I would be stronger. Because I wanted to be taken out of my depth.

But I also wanted to do it because I knew it would hurt. And I wanted it to hurt. I wanted to know what it felt like to show myself to someone other than him. *Other than him.* I wanted to stop thinking it was so precious. I wanted to be the one to do it before anyone else did. Before he forced me to see it.

Still, when I get home to my room, I feel so tired the only thing I can think to do is lie down on the bed.

So I do. I lie down and stare out the window at the HERBORISTE sign. And I remember the day Nise stood outside Baudon and said to me, *Il nous perturbe.* At the time I did not understand, not fully, but now I think I do.

And even when I tell myself *he* is not the one who disturbed me—that it was the day with Steven that disturbed me, and my own decision to unbutton my dress that disturbed me—I know those things are not the extent of the truth.

Because though I was the one who chose to go to Rue Taitbout, he was the one who gave me the choice, who opened the door.

Because it was from his photos that I knew how other girls posed.

Because from those photos I know what a person may buy.

Because it was his friend I went to see.

Because he was the reason I wanted to do something that hurt.

Because in the end, even though it was my choice, it was him that I wanted to please. Not Stevens. Not myself.

I think about all of that, and then I think about sitting for Stevens in his fancy studio, on a red velvet chair that was not old or worn but bright red and tight and rich. About how even the air in the studio felt different on my shoulders and neck. Softer. About how it was Stevens who was drawing me but it was him I was thinking of. Him. About his face and him touching me, kissing me between my legs and then drawing me.

It all runs together in my mind, and I feel adrift, as if the whole world is tilting away. I do not know what else to do, so I close my eyes to stop the spinning.

And when I open my eyes again, I look around. I look around and then I stand up and begin to touch things: my dresses hanging, the copper scarf from the whore that I keep spread on the table, the small watercolors I painted where my hair is green and my skin is blue. I touch the ribbon I stole from him, and the locket he gave. Last I touch the sketch he sent me and the envelope with my name on the front. *Mlle Victorine Louise Meurent, 32 Rue La Bruyère.* The sketch of the two of us together. The sketch of his cock rising into me.

I look around at everything until I cannot look anymore, and then I lie down on the bed again, and I let myself sleep.

Hours later, I wake up and take myself out to Raynal's for something to eat. Only when I have hot soup in my mouth and bread in my hand do I realize how much it took to allow Stevens to look at me. To allow myself to be seen by anyone except him.

When I get to Rue Guyot the next day, he is standing outside, across the street from the studio, smoking. Waiting and watching for me, the way he used to stand outside Baudon. At first I feel a rush of panic because he has never done it before, waited for me out in the street like that, and for a moment I think he must be angry. Angry somehow about yesterday. But when I get close and see the expression on his face, I understand it is nothing like that. Nothing at all like that.

He is standing outside because the work is done. The work on the scraped-away painting is done. For the moment, he has nothing more to do except wait for me.

When I get close to where he stands on the street, he draws one last time on the cigarette and then tosses it. Twists once with the toe of his shoe. The toss and the twist and reaching for me so he can kiss me on each cheek all happen in one motion, smoothly, like moves in a dance, even though we are there on the street.

"Did it pass your test?" I say. "The painting?"

"It did. And you, Trine? Ça va?"

So before I can decide not to, I say, "I went to see your friend yesterday."

"He told me. I saw him last night at Tortoni's."

He just stands there, looking at me, and when I see there is nothing to fear in his face, I can feel my shoulders go down. And even when I look away, I can feel him watching me.

"Was it hard then?" he asks. "To sit for him?"

"A little," I say. "Different from you."

I do not say it was nothing like being seen by him, that I felt lost afterward. À la dérive. But I think he must be able to tell. He must be able to tell from my face.

Still, all he says is, "I guess it would be."

We stand there for a moment, feeling the air in the street, and then he tells me, "You don't have to please people, you know."

I do not say anything—I just look at his face, which is not kind the way Stevens's face is, and is not a pool I can step into. His face is lean, and the plum shadows underneath his eyes are darker than ever.

"Make people please you," he tells me.

And when he says that, I know Stevens said something to him. Maybe not all of it, but something.

"Make them please you," he says again. "Make them work for it."

And I think about the way he kneels on the floor beside the

divan. The way he insists that I go before he does so he can feel it. So he can watch it. I think about the sign we saw one of the first nights we were together. *Demandez du Plaisir.*

"The way you work for it," I say.

"The way I work for it."

We look at each other then and do not turn away, either of us. I can feel the whole world tilting again. Can feel myself being pulled out of my level again. But I want it. I want to be taken out of my level. And I want him. And for him to know how much.

"Come on," he says. And he takes my hand, there in the street. And we walk into his studio together.

⟶

When I see the painting, everything from yesterday drops away. The feeling of tilting, the way I felt when I came back to my room—it all falls away.

There is only the painting. Only it.

I am almost life-size. That is the first thing I am not expecting. I do not know why—I saw the scraped canvas the first day, and the back of the canvas every day I lay on the divan. I knew he was working on something large. But seeing the back did not help me understand the effect of the painting itself. Its presence, or how it seems to fill the room.

"It's huge," I say. When it comes out, I realize how rude it sounds, so I say, "I'm sorry. It's different from what I thought it would be."

"What did you think it would be?"

"I didn't think I would fill the space," I say. Because I take up almost the entire painting. My body takes up the canvas. The sketches and ink washes were all smaller, but even that does not get at what I want to say. When I saw the scraped-down canvas, the body did not fill the space. How could it?

"It's almost as if you can touch me," I tell him. "I'm right there, all of me."

When I look at the hand that he agonized over, it looks exactly right to me. I don't know how a hand can look as if it wants to move, but that is how my hand looks in his painting. As if it wants to seek out the soft cleft between my legs again.

It is only after I make sense of the hand that I can look closely at the face in the painting. The face that looks directly out. That challenges. That shows the impatience of the hand.

My face.

Except the face in this painting does not look anything like the face in the portrait he painted of me, the one where my hair was pulled back and dirty. It does not look like that portrait of the drawing he did of me squatting in front of him. It does not even look like my face in Moulin's photographs.

Yet it is me.

I recognize myself.

I know the painting is me because I was here every day with him. But it is the first time I understand that what he puts in the paint is not only something different from what I am, but also something different from what he sees in me.

The painting has a life of its own.

"It's me but it's more than I am," I say.

"It's what it needs to be."

"You made it different from the other ones, too."

"The Titian?"

"All of them," I say. "The snake-woman with a curved back. Her face was a long white bone."

"The face on the Odalisque is a mask."

"It's a snob's face," I tell him. "This is a working girl's face. You gave her a working girl's face."

When he does not answer, I say, "Can't you see it? You're the one who did it. It's in her chin, in that little shadow under her chin. You made her real. She isn't me but she's like me."

He looks at the painting for a long time then without saying anything. Without looking at me. So I think I must have said the wrong thing.

"I don't know," I tell him. "It's just how I see it."

"No," he says, and his voice is full of some kind of emotion. That is when I see he feels moved by something.

"You should do it, you know," he tells me. "You should keep up with your drawing and painting. You have the eye of an artist."

When he says that, I do not know which one of us is more upset.

So we do the thing we know to do, which is to lie down together. It is what comes next. It is what we really are, anyway.

The root of everything.

When we get up from the divan, we go and stand in front of the painting again. I think he is still worked up when he tells me the next thing: that when the painting sells, he wants to give me a share.

"You've earned it," he says. "More than earned it. It will help you. You can do what you like with the money."

"You pay me each week to model," I say.

"For your work. For your time. This will be at a different level."

"When it happens we'll talk about it."

"Bien. But it's a contract and I want you to hold me to it."

I know it is his way, to talk about money and contracts. And I appreciate it, I do. But right now I want to tell him that I have fallen in love with the face he painted. I want to say I love her face the way I loved Nise's face. That I love whoever it is on the canvas. Me and not-me. But I do not say any of those things. I cannot talk about Nise or about love or about what I feel for him.

So I reach out to the painting, as if I am going to touch it. "I understand her," I tell him. "I understand who she is."

"Yes," he says. "I thought you would."

Acknowledgments

To my agent Nicole Aragi; editor Jill Bialosky at W. W. Norton; and Dominique Bourgois at Christian Bourgois Éditeur—thank you for believing in Victorine and me. Thank you also to Cécile Deniard, my French translator.

The story of how the gardener Guichet murdered the prostitute Mezeray is true; I learned about it and much more regarding the lives of working class women from Jill Harsin's *Policing Prostitution in Nineteenth-Century Paris*. *Poor & Pregnant in Paris: Strategies for Survival in the Nineteenth Century* by Rachel G. Fuchs also illuminated this topic. The story of a perfumer named Monpelas, killed by soldiers of Louis Napoleon in 1851, is also true and reported by Victor Hugo in *Napoleon the Little* (*Napoléon le Petit*). Félix-Jacques Antoine Moulin was a real Parisian photographer; I learned about him primarily through Serge Nazarieff's *Early Erotic Photography*.

In writing this novel, I spent hours looking at Charles Marville's photographs of Paris and the 1860 Andriveau-Goujon map of Paris. Even though historian Richard Cobb and photographer Nicholas Breach recorded a much more modern Paris in *The Streets of Paris* (1980), that book mattered deeply to me. I also studied medical photographs of men and women with syphilis taken by Oscar G. Mason and E. K. Hough; the photographs were featured in George Henry Fox's *Photographic Illustrations of Cutaneous Syphilis*, published in 1881.

And of course I read many books and articles on Victorine Meurent and Édouard Manet. For Victorine Meurent, Margaret Mary Armbrust Seibert's *A Biography of Victorine-Louise Meurent and Her Role in the Art of Edouard Manet* and Eunice Lipton's *Alias Olympia* were crucial. For Manet, I lived with (and often slept beside) the following books: Antonin Proust's *Édouard Manet: Souvenirs*; Françoise Cachin's *Manet: The Influence of the Modern*; Beth Archer Brombert's *Edouard Manet: Rebel in a Frock Coat*; Beatrice Farwell's *Manet and the Nude: A Study in Iconography in the Second Empire*; Robert Gordon and Andrew Forge's *The Last Flowers of Manet* (with translations from the French by Richard Howard); T. A. Gronberg's *Manet: A Retrospective*; and the Metropolitan Museum of Art's *Manet: 1832–1883*.

Please visit www.parisredblog.com for more background on the novel.

Mokena Community
Public Library District